ONLY

A BREATH

AWAY

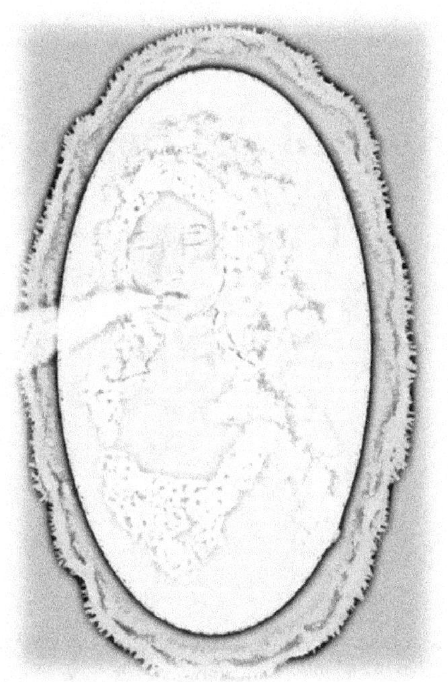

BY

PATTY RONCHETTO

Thank you to

Charlene Howard for the cover design

and to

Charlene Howard and Debbie Matusovic

for editing.

This book was printed in the United States of America.

Copyright © 2020 Patty Ronchetto

ISBN: 9798634265407
Imprint: Independently published

TABLE OF CONTENTS

The Victorian Mirror

PART ONE

Chapter One

My curiosity was launched once I set eyes on that aged rarity, an heirloom from the Victorian era. It was an oval shaped mirror that was ornate but not gaudy. A golden flower vine scrolled around the slightly chipped ivory colored frame. I had no idea why I wanted this mirror or even where I would put it in my home, it simply seemed to beckon to me.

I asked Henry, the antiques dealer, to hold it for me so I could find my friends to show them. My two friends, Lexi and Donna, were up on the third floor of this antiques mall looking for small furniture items. I was on the main floor visiting with Henry when my eye caught the hanging mirror. I never liked rummaging through other people's things so I wasn't enthralled with antique shopping. Most items in such stores were kitsch, or junk. Occasionally, it was fun to reminisce whenever I came across a <u>Fun with Dick and Jane</u> book, Campbell's memorabilia, or toys and dolls similar to those I had owned as a child, however, the repetition of such items and the identical mildew odor in every antiques shop kept it from being a favorite hobby of mine.

I tracked down my two friends. They were thrilled I was showing some interest in a possible antique acquisition and were happy to give me their opinion. Donna was the one most interested in antiques, but only those that were in almost flawless condition resulting in a steep price. Donna tended to spend money that we often wondered where and if she had such funds.

I wasn't surprised Donna's reaction was kind of derogatory, "Oh," she stared at the mirror. "That's it, huh? Where would you put that in your house? It's not in such great shape!"

Defending my interest, I replied, "Donna, it's over 100 years old and from the Victorian Era! Think of the history this mirror has seen."

Donna looked at me curiously, "You realize it's an inanimate object, don't you?"

Before I could respond, Lexi spoke up, "You know, it does have character. Has it been retouched at all?"

Henry, who was observing our discussion, chimed in, "Actually, the mirror glass is very clean and clear, perhaps re-silvered at some point. It is in surprisingly good condition. I would estimate it was made in the mid 1800's and is of French origin. The oval frame surrounding the glass has a scrolling floral design, and you can see there are a few chips in the plaster work. The gilt paint shows some wear and darkening in areas. It could be restored or just re-gilded. The wood back edge also shows wear. It has a metal hanging loop attached to the brown paper back that would have been added, as I believe the original mirror was displayed on an easel. It is quite a lovely piece."

Henry took out a measuring tape placing it gently on the mirror. "I only unpacked this mirror earlier today, so I don't have all the information documented yet. Let me get measurements for you. Including the frame, it is 28" in height, 16.5" in width, and only about an inch thick."

"I can see you buying that, Anna," Lexi said as she nodded. "Would you paint over it?"

Immediately Henry spoke up, "No, no, you don't want to do that. It would spoil the purpose of having such an item. It would also bring the value down."

"So, how much would that value cost Anna?" Donna's nature was to be slightly condescending and sarcastic.

Henry smiled, "Like I said, it just came in and I liked the piece so much I immediately put it on the wall. It is not yet priced, but I'm estimating we would mark it at $495.00. Anna, you said this would be your first purchase of an antique piece. We have gotten to know each other through the years of visiting with you while your friends explored my store. In honor of your first investment, it can be yours for $300.00. My hope is you may want to come back and purchase another piece from my store."

"Henry, do you have any record of the history of this particular mirror or any more details?" I was truly interested.

"I can check with my colleagues to obtain the provenance. That should tell us the origin and background, but it will take a few hours as we are still unloading the pieces."

When I looked at the mirror my stomach fluttered. Maybe it was hunger, maybe not. I knew I wanted that mirror but did not want to appear too eager.

"Henry, we were going to go get a bite to eat so could you hold it for me until after lunch?" I knew Donna would try to talk me out of it, and I wasn't sure about Lexi. The end result was it was my money, my decision. The girls and I had been coming on this annual trip for almost 30 years, and we always shared our opinions on such purchases over lunch.

"Sure, I can hold it for a few hours. Have a nice lunch."

We headed over to our favorite place to eat. Overlooking St. Croix River, The River's Edge, was rustic and casual. Through the years we tried other restaurants in Stillwater. They had good food but did not have the ambience that The River's Edge provided with windows all around so the view was captivating.

Once we were seated and had our iced tea ordered, Donna spoke up with concern, "Why don't you order an alcoholic drink? You can't stop drinking because of me. I can't avoid everyone I know who drinks."

Lexi smiled and said, "Donna, you know me. There are too many calories in alcohol."

I chuckled and commented, "I'm the driver this time and that is my excuse!"

"Well, as long as you aren't drinking because of me." Donna's eyes were downcast, looking dejected. "God only knows how badly I want a drink now, but I've only been four months sober."

Lexi and I exchanged a glance. In that glance we knew from all our years together that it would just be a matter of time before Donna would be in trouble again. Her years of coping from an abusive childhood and then never reaching her expected career goals had taken a toll on her. Her divorce had been fifteen years ago, but she dwelled on the hurt as if it was yesterday. It didn't help that Lexi and I were both happily married. Donna often displayed her jealousy.

Jumping in to change the subject, I rubbed my hands together excitedly with a wide grin on my face and said, "Let's discuss my pending purchase!"

They both rolled their eyes and chuckled.

Donna said, "It doesn't matter what we think, you're gonna buy it anyway!"

Lexi agreed but was supportive, "It will be interesting when Henry gets background details on the mirror. Maybe it belonged to a queen or some royalty."

"Well, if it did, just call me 'Queen Anna'." The mood was lightened, and we reviewed our plan for the rest of the day.

Chapter Two

Once we returned to the Stillwater Antiques Mall, Henry had the mirror wrapped and ready for me to take home. Unfortunately, he could not locate the provenance.

"Anna, I have some puzzling news about this piece." Henry removed his glasses and stroked his chin while contemplating his next words. "While you were at lunch, we finished unloading the shipment that your mirror was in. For some strange reason, the mirror is not listed on the shipment manifest. My colleagues and I have checked and cross-checked each item against the manifest and matched all documents with their appropriate items. The mirror wasn't listed, and there weren't any documents pertaining to it. This is very strange. I will need to do some checking with our overseas seller and get back to you."

"Does this mean I can't buy the mirror?" I asked. I was disheartened.

"Well, we don't sell you a piece that we deem to be an antique without providing a complete provenance listing all of the history and details. I offered you a deal on this piece, and my word is good. I can let you take the mirror home as is, however without the documented paperwork, if you were to resell it, we legally cannot acknowledge its authenticity. I will be happy to give you my hypothesis of the details on this piece, but it is simply my guess."

"I really want the mirror," I said to Henry. "If I take it now, would you continue to look for the documents?"

"Of course," Henry nodded adding, "It is highly unusual that this paperwork is missing. I am guessing the place of origin is France, the date of manufacture was circa 1850 — period mid-19th century — materials and techniques hand carved giltwood, gilt; condition excellent; wear consistent with age and use. I will continue to research and keep in contact with you."

Getting to know Henry over the years, I had no doubt I could trust him. He was one of the owners of this shop and quite a knowledgeable antiquarian. Henry was close to ninety years old but still as sharp as ever. Tall and lanky, he was in good shape, walking every day from his home a mile away. He was born and raised in this town and had no plans to leave his home. After his wife passed away a few years ago, his only child, a son, also in the antiques business, pleaded with him to sell his house and move to a senior center. Henry refused, stating as long as he was of sound mind and could continue to work, he would never leave his home. I pictured his house being stuffed with antiques and Henry tinkering with them when he was not at work.

"All right, Henry. I will write you a check, and we can keep in touch to learn any further details. Do you have any suggestions for how to clean this mirror?"

"Yes, I have already written it down for you and included it with the mirror when I wrapped it up. Basically, remember not to spray directly onto the mirror. You want to avoid re-silvering it as I mentioned earlier because it will decrease its value. Simply use one part rubbing alcohol or vinegar, to two parts water on a soft, lint free cloth. If you are doing more shopping, you can pick this up when you are done."

"Thank you, Henry. Donna and Lexi are purchasing some pieces too, so we will pick them up before we head home."

Donna found a cute little table. It was dark wood with spindle legs. There was a lower shelf and small drawer under the top. The top needed repair, but Donna planned on fixing the top with mosaic tile and putting the table in her bathroom.

Lexi picked up some old books. One was an early edition of <u>Les Misérables</u>, which the three of us had seen three times at the Orpheum Theatre in downtown Minneapolis.

Leaving Stillwater, we made our usual stop at the Dairy Queen outside of town. This was our dessert, a chocolate dipped cone. Driving back to the city, we reminisced on our day. We each bought a variety of oils and vinegars at the Olive Oil Store. The Christmas Store was one of our favorite places. It was open year-round, and as we all loved Christmas, it was a given we would stop there. All three of us owned Christmas village sets and usually bought the newest house edition on this trip. This year I passed on it as I spent more than I planned on the mirror, and I had to admit, as I age, it was getting too tiring to drag out all the Christmas houses, arrange them, replace light bulbs and cords, and then, after just about a month, pack them back into storage.

"Anna, where do you think you will hang your mirror?" Lexi asked.

"I've been thinking about that. I don't need another mirror in my bedroom. I just don't know." I was pondering where the best location would be.

"How about the bathroom?" Donna suggested.

"I don't think you should hang it there as too much steam could affect it," Lexi stated. Then she yelled, "I got it! You have that long hallway leading to the bedrooms. It would fit perfectly on the wall at the end of the hall."

I contemplated that suggestion and smiled. "Yes, that would be a perfect place. I have a small table there now with a picture of flowers on that wall, but I'm tired of that picture. Thank you, Lexi. That's where it will go!"

Donna agreed.

Once I arrived home after dropping the girls off with their treasures, I gently removed the mirror from my car and brought it inside the house. My husband, Joe, was home. Joe and I had an understanding. Our mortgage was finally paid off. We both worked hard all of our lives and had pensions. The money we drew each month from Social Security was contributed to the household fund for groceries, utilities, improvements, insurance, etc. Anything left over went into our joint savings account for vacations and fun things. Our pension money was ours to spend as we pleased. Joe had interests in sports and guns. He enjoyed going to the shooting range weekly, and he often invested in different games like fantasy football and basketball with many of his friends. My interests included going to plays and musicals and lunching with friends. I also enjoyed making my own greeting cards.

As I unwrapped the mirror, I asked Joe what he thought.

"Well, it depends how much it cost," he said with some uncertainty.

"Joe, it's an antique from the 19th century!" I exclaimed.

Joe simply chuckled saying, "They saw you coming."

I didn't care! I carried it down the hall, removed the flower picture and hung the mirror in its place. It looked good, like it belonged there. The only problem was lighting. Unless the overhead light in the hallway was turned on, the darkness of the area made it difficult to see my newest purchase. The mirror hung a little crooked. I took it down to see what I could adjust on the back to have it hang straight. I remember Henry said he believed originally the mirror was placed on an easel and the wiring for hanging was added later. I carried the mirror to the dining room table, turned it over, and contemplated what I could do to correct the problem.

There was the slightest bulge under the brown paper on one side. I rubbed my finger over the bump noticing it was different from the area directly across it. The more I examined it I realized it was not just a small area as it covered the length of the mirror on the one side. This would explain the skewed hanging. I didn't want to cut into what was beneath this brown paper covering. The wire for hanging the mirror was attached by two old brass screw eyes, one on each side. I decided to remove one, but as hard as I tried, I could not budge either one. I called Joe in to help me. He got his pliers. I cautioned him to be careful. It took some time and lots of grit on his part, but the screw finally pivoted. He suggested we remove both screw eyes and maybe use a razor blade to slice into the brown paper backing and try to slide out whatever was in there. My nervousness was apparent as I was rapidly pacing. I asked Joe to perform the necessary surgery as I was too jumpy. Maybe it was the certificate of authenticity or maybe something else, something secretive! Once the screw eyes were removed, he took a razor blade and made a neat slice in the paper. I grabbed a tweezer from the bathroom and asked him to use it to pull out whatever was inside. Slowly, an old yellowed paper, similar to a parchment texture was removed. The paper was folded about four times length-wise. Joe handed it to me to open.

I was amazed to find a letter dated June 15th, 1837. It had been written in script and what appeared to be ink, slightly smudged.

Back then, it was most likely written with a quill, dipped in an ink well.

15th of June, 1837

My Beloved,
You cried when we held each other

and professed our love together.

Entwined in our arms, we tasted the sweetness of our love,

But it was fleeting like the wings of a dove.

In dreams alone, our love will always remain,

As the reign is near and duty causes much pain.

Be happy, my beloved, remember this,

No regrets to take amiss.

In Heaven again we will meet someday,

And share the love that will return our way.

I was so excited to find such a treasure but in reading this love poem it brought up so many other questions like who wrote this letter, who received it, was this a secretive affair, was it a suicide note, and why was it hidden? I couldn't wait to show it to Lexi and Donna. Tomorrow I would call Henry, too. I'm sure he would want to see it. I had to be careful as the paper seemed crumbly.

Joe now seemed more interested in the letter than in the mirror, going on and on about finding out how much money the letter could be worth.

I was interested in discovering the secrets behind the letter hidden in the mirror. I carefully placed the letter in a large manila envelope and couldn't wait to find out more.

Chapter Three

Joe and I carefully replaced the screw eyes and wire so we could hang the mirror back on the wall. Unable to have a restful sleep wondering about the love poem hidden in the mirror, I got up at 6:00 am and made a pot of coffee. Realizing it was too early to call Lexi, Donna, and Henry, I waited for Joe to get up, get dressed, and have breakfast with me. Staring at the wall and cupboards that we updated before Joe and I retired, I felt a sense of contentment. When we bought this house, the kitchen was wallpapered with yellow and white polka dots. The cupboards were dark brown wood, definitely in need of work. The brass handles on the cupboards didn't all match and some were missing screws. We did a complete remodeling with all matching stainless-steel appliances, including the sink. After the wallpaper was taken down and the walls were prepped, we painted them a colonial blue. The woodwork was painted white. We decided to paint the cupboards white but remove the fronts. They were replaced with glass fronts, trimmed in white. The floor that had been a shabby brown was now white and gray tile that coordinated nicely with the countertops. We chose a granite counter top with scroll work of white, gray, and blue. Joe and I knew remodeling a kitchen would be costly but as we planned on staying in this house for as long as we could, we wanted it to be updated. I loved my new kitchen. It now was so airy and open. A window over the sink looked out on our small but beautifully landscaped backyard, another hobby of Joe's. In my bright and airy kitchen, I read the poem over and over.

By the time Joe made an appearance, I must have reread that poem fifty times, trying to dissect it line by line, wondering if there were any hidden meanings in the words. The lines that I kept going back to were:

"As the reign is near and duty causes much pain,"

and

"In Heaven again we will meet someday,

And share the love that will return our way."

With the year written on the poem being 1837 and if this was in France, I decided to Google France during that time. France was in turmoil then. The Victorian era from 1837 to 1901 was a period of extreme social inequality and deep and sustained religious revival. My interest peaked at an online article stating it was a golden age of belief in supernatural forces, energies, and phenomena. This could be the result that advances in science were so rapid, the natural and supernatural often became blurred in popular thinking. It was the time of the Industrial Revolution. The inventions of the telegraph, telephone, and light bulb were only a few. The telegraph, invented in 1837, soon became obsolete after only 39 years with the invention of the telephone. The article further read that rapid evolving lead to dehumanization of work, child labor, pollution, and growth of cities where poverty, filth, and disease flourished. Some of this sounded like the present time. Maybe history does repeat itself.

That was as far as I read before Joe joined me in the kitchen. I told him about my morning so far and all he said was, "What does that have to do with your mirror?"

"Nothing, I guess, I simply wanted to see what was happening during that time. There is a lot more to read about the era."

Joe looked at me and shook his head, "I think you're wasting time and getting your hopes up. Just call Henry."

"You're right. I'll wait until 9:00 to do that. Hopefully he will be at the store then."

Joe left to run errands, and I impatiently sat at the kitchen table with my laptop and way too much coffee to be calm. I got up and walked around the wall separating the kitchen from the hallway and living room. I stood at the furthest end of the hallway facing the mirror. Paraphrasing a line from "Sleeping Beauty", I whispered, "Mirror, mirror, on the wall, where did you come from? Who did you belong to?"

Nothing. Of course, nothing. What did I expect?

It was almost 9:00 am, and I first called Lexi and Donna. They were both astonished and wanted to come over right away to see the poem written over a century ago. Donna volunteered to bring lunch over that afternoon.

Next, I called Henry. He was still unable to find any information on the mirror, however, he did have a phone message into the seller in France and expected to hear from them at any time, but knew it would depend on the time difference. Relaying my discovery to Henry, he wanted to see the letter right away. I told him I understood but I could not drive up to Stillwater for a few days. Stillwater was an hour and a half drive from my house. Henry, almost ninety years old, no longer drove. He asked if I would mind if his son, Phillip, who lived in St. Paul, came to my house to examine the letter. Feeling more comfortable with that, I agreed. I didn't want my discovery to break down from outside elements with so many people handling it.

Henry's son called about an hour later. He would be at my house that evening to examine the letter and also wanted to see the mirror.

I straightened up the kitchen in anticipation of my luncheon with Lexi and Donna. It didn't take long, so I poured myself another cup of coffee. Sitting in silence, I thought I heard a whirring noise, like wind blowing but as I looked out the window, no leaves on trees were moving, nothing was swaying from wind. Getting up from the table with my coffee in hand, I slowly meandered around the kitchen wall back to the hall. I stood in front of the mirror as a shadow seemed to cross passed it. Looking behind me, there wasn't anyone or anything that would have caused such a shadow. I wish it was brighter in the hallway, but how could I have seen a shadow without much lighting? The whirring noise got louder and suddenly the mirror surface started rippling. I screamed! My coffee cup slipped out of my hand, shattering on the wooden floor with coffee splattering on the wall and floor. I stared at the mirror but as my eyes focused on it, the rippling subsided, and it was silent once again.

Chapter Four

I stood there frozen with my mouth open, afraid to move, but nothing happened. After several minutes, I picked up the pieces of the broken cup, grabbed some paper towels from the kitchen, and wiped up the spilled coffee all while continually turning my head to stare at the mirror. Did I imagine what just happened? Maybe I was tired from being up so early and rereading the letter so many times. It must have been my imagination.

A little unnerved, I was shaking and needed to calm down. Deciding to sit outside on my front porch in the white wooden rocker, I read the newspaper to keep my mind occupied on something else. It was a warm and bright morning, and the sun felt good on my face. There wouldn't be many autumn days like this left before the snow rolled in, so I wanted to take advantage of it.

I must have nodded off as the honking of a horn startled me. It was Donna and Lexi. Oh my God, was it was lunch time already? Actually, it was only 10:30, but the girls were so excited to see the letter. They couldn't wait. Donna decided instead of bringing lunch over, she would order pizza for all of us.

First, I showed them where the mirror was hanging, not mentioning anything about my earlier sensation as I didn't know if it was real. The mirror, being 28" in length, hung at my eye level. Both Donna and Lexi were slightly taller than my 5'2" frame so when they looked into the mirror they saw more of their neck and upper body clothing.

"I wish the mirror had been a full-length mirror," Donna mentioned as she inspected it. "Maybe it would be clearer. It seems kind of hazy, doesn't it?"

"Funny you should say that as I imagined a little while ago it was actually making a noise and rippling." I laughed and decided to confide in them about what I thought I had witnessed.

"What kind of a noise?" Lexi asked.

"A whirring noise like the wind blowing or the noise an ocean would make."

"What? Are you insane?" Donna accused.

"Don't be so quick to make fun, Donna," Lexi interjected. "After all, the origin of the mirror is still a mystery."

"Well, mystery or not, let's go into the kitchen, and I will show you the love poem."

I had to admit that even Donna was at a loss for words. I asked them to please be careful as the paper was somewhat compromised.

"Have you spoken with Henry about this?" Lexi asked, somewhat dumbfounded.

"Yes, his son, Phillip, lives in St. Paul. Apparently, Phillip has an antiques shop in the city and will be coming over tonight to inspect both the letter and the mirror."

"Leave it to you, Anna. You never liked antiques, never even made a purchase. Then, you decide on the fly to buy one, and it is quite the mystery and probably worth a lot of money!"

"Oh, stop," Lexi tapped Donna's shoulder giving her a slight shove. "Don't you think this is exciting!"

"Of course, I do."

"Well, girls, let's not get ahead of ourselves before we know what is what. All Joe wants to know is how much money the letter could be worth." We all laughed.

Lexi, who loved to read historical romantic novels, was deep in thought. Tapping her index finger against the side of her face she said,

"What if the poem was written to Queen Victoria by her secret lover! The timing would be right."

"I doubt if anything Queen Victoria ever owned would end up in an antiques shop in Stillwater, Minnesota," Donna smirked.

"Oh my God," I spoke louder than I meant to. "Look at the lines in the poem. It mentions 'reign' as in the reign of royalty. It also mentions 'duty causes much pain' and that could refer to wartime."

I then told them of my earlier findings on the internet when I searched the time period.

"OK, get that laptop open again, Anna, we've got more research to do," Lexi said eagerly.

Donna shook her head saying, "First I'm calling in our pizza order. You gals are wasting time. Just let Henry's son figure it out."

Just then, I heard the noise again. The girls did too. We ran into the hallway and stared at the rippling mirror.

Chapter Five

A gasp came from Lexi as her hand flew to cover her opened mouth. Donna's face had gone pale, almost ashen, staring with wide open eyes and unaware she had grabbed Lexi's arm. I stood there with my arms crossed in front of me and my fingernails piercing into the flesh of my upper arms. The whirring noise was sounding clearer now. It almost sounded like someone trying to whisper and then the mirror stopped. We all stood silent for several minutes, my legs weak and shaking, not knowing what to do. I felt like we must have all been in a hypnotic state staring straight ahead.

Donna broke the silence by saying, "I can't believe this," over and over again while shaking her head. Lexi looked like she was in shock, staring at the mirror without blinking.

Trying to calm everyone, including myself, I placed my arms around Lexi turning her around, facing the opposite direction of the mirror. Donna's eyes met mine, and she kept shaking her head.

"Let's go into the kitchen and discuss what just happened." I didn't know why I was whispering, I just knew I wanted to get away from the mirror.

Once we sat down and after moments of silent disbelief, Donna started in again muttering, "I can't believe this."

I was worried about Lexi but she finally spoke, "It was almost like the noise was someone trying to speak."

She finally looked at me. Disbelief was still evident in her rapidly blinking eyes, but I did not see any signs of shock.

"Could you decipher anything from the noise?" I asked.

"It was like someone whispering, 'HELP'". Lexi covered her face with her hands and shook her head. After a while she put her hands down and looked at me seriously, asking, "What was that?"

Before I could respond, Donna broke in with mocking laughter, "OK, where is Joe? You two are trying to pull a fast one on us. Is there a battery behind that mirror to make it ripple? How did you make that sound?"

"Joe and I haven't done anything. Joe doesn't even know about this. The first time it happened I was home alone this morning. Joe wouldn't play such a trick on me."

"Hmph!" Donna grunted. She got up to call in the pizza order that was previously interrupted by the noise of the mirror.

Lexi and I sat in silence, both in our own skeptical thoughts. Donna joined us at the table as I let out a big sigh and softly said, "At least you were here to see that so you won't think I'm going crazy."

The three of us looked at each other and together let out a nervous laugh.

"I'm not sold on this nonsense," Donna said almost trying to convince herself more than anyone. "I want to take a look at that mirror!"

With that, Donna got up from the table, went into the hall and stared, scrutinizing the mirror. Lexi and I cautiously followed. As Donna placed her hands on the mirror in an effort to remove it from the wall, she jumped back while her voice let out a high-pitched shriek.

I ran over to her asking if she was OK. Lexi stayed back, still hesitant at how close she should get to the mirror.

"I got a shock! The mirror felt so hot!" Donna exclaimed. "What in the hell is that thing?"

"Hopefully, that's what Phillip can tell me tonight."

We sat in silence until the pizza arrived without any further noise from the mirror.

"I'm afraid," Lexi murmured. "I don't want to be here with that, that, 'THING.'"

"It is a little unsettling," Donna replied, "but I think there has to be some kind of scientific and logical explanation."

"I don't care! I can't stay here! I'm sorry, Anna."

"Don't be sorry, Lexi, I'm as mystified as you girls, and yes, afraid too. Let's go out onto the deck for lunch. I'm hoping Joe will be home soon. Maybe he can figure it out."

Joe made it home in time to finish off the pizza that was left, which was quite a bit, as none of us felt much like eating. As he entered the back deck and sat down to join us, he asked, "What's going on? And what **is** that noise in the house? Is that why you're

eating out here?"

Chapter Six

Like Donna, Joe's practical self, thought it was a joke when we relayed the morning happenings. After many attempts at trying to convince him of what we experienced, I think it was Lexi who finally had him concerned. "I can't go back in there, Joe, and I won't go back in there." Lexi was now biting her nails, a quirk I had never seen her do.

Joe could tell she was truly frightened. "All right, I'm going to go in and take a look at it."

As we anxiously waited outside, the only sound we heard was a few birds chirping. It didn't take long before Joe came back, sat down on our picnic table, and shook his head, "It's a mystery to me."

"What, Joe, what? Did you hear it? Was it still hot?" I almost screamed the questions to him.

"Well, it wasn't making noise any longer, but it was warm. I didn't get zapped. I'm thinking maybe it was some kind of glass or metal reflection but there are no windows or other mirrors around it to create such an illusion. It's in the dark hallway!"

"But you did hear the noise when you came home, right, Joe?" I reiterated.

"I heard something when I entered the house. I can't swear it came from the mirror. Did you contact Henry?"

"Yes, his son, Phillip, is coming by this evening to examine the poem and the mirror."

The girls were ready to leave. Lexi asked Donna to get her purse from inside the house as she would not go back in.

"I'm sorry, Anna, it's nothing personal, I'm just petrified of what we experienced in there."

"Stop apologizing, Lexi, I don't blame you at all. There must be a reason as to what happened in there and I hope Henry's son will provide us with an explanation."

The three of us said our goodbyes and hugged each other harder and longer than usual. I promised to let them know of Phillip's findings.

The house remained calm for the next several hours. Phillip arrived at 4:00 p.m. After introductions, I told him about the antics this mirror seemed to possess. Surprisingly, he did not look at me like I was nuts. He simply nodded while stroking his beard. He then asked the strangest question, "How well do you know my father?"

I was taken back but replied that I had visited him at his store for many years, however, this had been my first purchase. "Why do you ask, Phillip?"

"Just wondering. I would like to see the letter now."

"Okay." I was thinking Phillip did not seem to have much of a personality.

He had brought in a black satchel. He set it on the kitchen table alongside the letter. Phillip withdrew latex gloves from his bag along with some small equipment. He put his gloves on and set out a few extra pairs cautioning us not to allow anyone to touch the letter without wearing these gloves. It seemed like forever that he perused the letter, turning it over and over, studying the script and ink through what he described as a miniature microscope and small infrared light.

"Would it be possible for me to take the letter to my office to perform some chemical tests?"

I looked at Joe. He shrugged his shoulders. I was struggling with this. "Phillip, I really don't know you, and I don't want you to think I don't trust you, but if this letter is real and is worth a lot of money, what assurance do I have that you will return it to me?"

"I understand. I apologize I did not give you my card when I came in. He handed both Joe and me his card. His title was "curator" and "owner" of a shop called "The Art of Antiquity".

"I didn't know you owned your shop. I thought you worked there."

"Well, I own it with my friend from college. His name is Mark. We both attended college out east in New York, where we met. My undergraduate degree is in Archival Science with my masters in Art History. I am the Curator of our business and Mark is the Archivist as his master's degree was in Archival Studies. We make a good team."

I could feel the warmness of embarrassment rise up my neck to my face. "I apologize, Phillip, I didn't realize how knowledgeable you were. Your father didn't tell me anything about you other than you worked at an antiques shop in St. Paul."

Joe cut in saying, "Phillip, sometimes my wife has trust issues. Please don't take it personally."

"No problem. I can tell you what I 'think' your letter is but it would be better if you would allow me to have Mark do a detailed paper analysis which would involve some chemical testing. I would certainly give you a letter of guarantee stating the poem and its authenticity would be returned to you upon completion. By paying me for the testing, that is another guarantee.

Let me explain what I know so far:

1. The content of the letter must correspond to its time period. In this case, at first observation, I believe it does.

2. The materials and techniques must be consistent with the place and time. I believe the technique is more in the 1800's than the 1900's. I cannot confirm the material, meaning the ink, without a chemical analysis. For example, if an analysis shows that more than one pen was used, or more than one ink type, we would conclude the letter had been traced. The parchment looks authentic but

again, an analysis would need to be done to authenticate that.

3. The method of printing would be easier to decipher if there were stamps or seals, however, this letter does not have any. A seal of some kind would help immensely to determine family crests or royalty."

"Wow, I didn't realize there was so much involved. Of course, I will let you take the letter with you." I was still feeling a pang of embarrassment.

Joe interjected, "How much would this analysis and authentication cost us?"

"Mark and I each charge between $150 to $300 per hour, depending upon the extent of identifying and classifying such items. Once Mark sees the item, I will be able to give you a better idea. I can certainly call you beforehand to provide a better estimate before you are committed.   Now, I would like to see the mirror that the letter was hidden in."

The three of us walked into the hallway. The mirror was not making any noise.

"Well, it looks guiltless enough," Phillip said with a smirk. "Do you mind if I remove it from the wall so I can study the framing?"

I quickly looked at Joe, remaining silent. After a few quiet seconds, Joe responded, "Of course not. Go ahead."

Oh, sure, I thought, Joe still does not believe me.

Phillip approached the mirror and as he attempted to remove it from the nail on the wall, he was zapped falling right down on his derriere.

"I was wrong," he said, with amazement in his eyes.

Chapter Seven

It was obvious the mirror would remain on our wall. Once I hung the mirror, somehow it attached and sealed itself like a stamp adhered to an envelope. A coldness of fear penetrated through me. I did not like the idea of this strange phenomenon remaining in my home, taking hold of me.

The three of us remained silent for several minutes. Phillip broke the silence,

"Anna, I am amazed! We are dealing with something I cannot explain, at least, not now. I would like to bring my partner, Mark, over here so we can examine it together. I will not charge you for this examination as my curiosity needs to be satisfied. My interest and education of such a piece will be payment enough."

Joe and I agreed to Phillip's proposal. I stressed to him how I wanted this done as soon as possible as I felt uneasy sleeping in this house with the mirror, or whatever it was. Phillip left with the letter, which he carefully placed in plastic and put in his bag. He promised to call me the next morning after he had spoken to Mark.

Joe and I were quiet most of the evening, each in our own thoughts of the object that had taken up permanent residence in our home. Joe kept repeating,

"There has got to be some reasonable or scientific explanation."

I didn't know what to think. We went to bed early, not knowing if we would fall asleep. I turned the television on in our bedroom. Usually the TV helps Joe fall asleep within ten minutes. I am the night owl, flipping channels to watch old shows from the fifties and sixties or CNN until about 1:00 or 2:00 am. It was about midnight when I heard the soft, puffy breathing of Joe, lightly snoring. I finished watched "Everybody Loves Raymond" and at 1:00 am I turned the TV off.

*   *   *

I woke with a start, ending the strange dream I was having. The clock read 3:30 am. Sitting up, I recalled my dream. I was wearing a huge, dirty, white house dress, not fancy at all, more like an oversized, unattractive uniform. My hair was in a bun on top of my head, covered with an off-white cotton cap with ruffles around its edges. I was on my hands and knees, scrubbing a massive, beautiful mosaic floor. It was beige with green, red, and blue tile pieces intersecting each other, seeming like the floor never ended and I would never finish this task. As I continued scrubbing, I felt severe sharp abdominal pains. Looking down at my stomach, I was shocked and could not believe my eyes! My God, I must have been nine months pregnant! I screamed in pain as a trickle of bright, red blood flowed down to the bottom of my dress turning the white

34

material crimson and staining the floor I had just scoured. It was then I woke up. I sat in bed for a few minutes with Joe sound asleep, oblivious to my nightmare.

I got up to get a glass of water and checked myself to be sure there was no blood. There was no sign so I knew it was just a strange dream. I tried to shake the dream from my mind. Sipping from my glass of water, I felt an urge or force that seemed to beckon me to visit the mirror in the hallway.

Carefully, I walked toward the mirror. It started rippling again. I felt mesmerized. A woman's face appeared in the mirror. I could not scream! Spellbound, unable to utter a word, it was like I was transfixed, unable to do anything except stand there and listen.

She appeared to be in her early twenties. Dark brown hair strands fell down the side of her face and most of her hair was nestled on her head, probably in a bun, as a white cap covered it so I didn't know for sure. The cap on her head resembled the same one I wore in my dream. Tears clouded her eyes as she finally spoke,

"Please help me, ma'am. They took my baby!" she pleaded.

I must still be sleeping! Maybe I was sleep walking and this was all a crazy dream! I still couldn't move. It felt like I was frozen to the floor.

"Please ma'am, find my baby. I know she didn't die like they said. They took her! Oh, please," she begged.

Suddenly, I became aware of my surroundings and knew I was awake. Can't Joe hear this, I thought? As I stood rigidly, this person's face, or reflection in the mirror, started moving, like the rippling I had experienced earlier. Slowly, limb by limb, my body seemed to warm up, and I could once again move and then, she was gone.

Chapter Eight

It was still the middle of the night and difficult to comprehend what had just happened. Not wanting to wake up Joe yet, I quietly crawled into bed. What the hell was that? Could a person's imagination make up visions that seem so real? But what about the others who heard and witnessed the rippling of the mirror? What about Phillip unsuccessfully trying to remove it from the wall? The shocks this mirror gave people made me feel it could be evil. Then again, the image of the woman asking for her baby was heart wrenching. I started to ponder that my dream was somehow related to this. After all, in my dream I was in full-term pregnancy and then there was the blood. And the cap she wore was the same as I wore in my dream! Shivers crept down my back as thoughts of the image in the mirror may be a ghost trying to contact me for help. But why me? And what was it about this mirror in that Stillwater antiques shop that made me want it so bad? Joe would worry about my mental state if I engaged him in the conversation I was having with myself, so I decided to confide in Phillip and his partner. Finally drifting off to sleep, I had a much needed peaceful and uneventful slumber.

*   *   *

"Wake up, honey," Joe was gently shaking my shoulder to wake me.

"Phillip is on the phone."

I threw the covers off me, attempting to get my bearings.

"You are quite the sleepy head today. You never sleep this late! Are you feeling OK?" Joe was sincerely concerned for me.

"What time is it?" I asked, still in somewhat of a fog.

"It's 10:00 am. Here Phillip wants to talk to you." Joe handed me my cell phone. It had been right next to me on my bedside table but I never heard it ring.

"Hello Phillip." I knew I sounded sleepy.

"Sorry to wake you."

"Oh, no, don't be. I never sleep this late. I'm usually the first one up."

"Anna, I don't want to inconvenience you, but after I discussed the situation with Mark, I also phoned my dad. I found out some information. Would it be OK if Mark and I came over today?"

"Yes, actually I was going to call you this morning as I witnessed something else with the mirror, and I need help understanding what this is or how to get it out of my house!" I was desperate, silently recollecting the encounter last night.

"Hang on, Anna, we can be over before noon if that's OK with you and Joe?"

Of course, it was. I asked Joe if he had heard noise of any kind from the hallway where the mirror was, and he had not. Joe had already made coffee so I showered to clear the lethargy I was feeling.

*   *   *

Phillip and Mark arrived just a few minutes before noon. Mark was anxious to see the mirror. We stepped into the hallway. We remained quiet while Mark scrutinized the mirror from a short distance. He pulled out a sketch pad and pencil from his briefcase and started sketching. When he was finished, he nodded to us and said, "Let's talk in the living room."

Joe played host getting all of us coffee and water. I sat on the couch with Mark while Phillip stood listening intently.

"This is quite remarkable," Mark began. "I have only seen one other mirror with the antique characteristics similar to this one. It was many years ago when I was vacationing in Europe after my college graduation. I was touring a castle outside of Paris, France. It was the Chateau de Chantilly or Chantilly Castle. It is an exquisite part of French history. It dates back to the mid to late 19th century when it was rebuilt, as the original castle was destroyed during the French Revolution. This castle never belonged to any French

39

royalty, but was always in the possession of noble families. The mirror I saw was in the servants' quarters of the castle."

"Do you think this could be that mirror?" I asked.

"I don't believe so. I mean, it was many years ago, but the reason I sketched it today is Phillip explained to me the shock he received in trying to remove it from the wall. That triggered my memory of my time in Europe. I looked through my old picture albums and there was a snapshot I took in the servants' quarters. Here, let me show you, I brought it with me."

He pulled the picture out of his briefcase and remarked, "You can see the edging is different but basically it looks similar. If it was a different color, I would think it could be your mirror; however, as you can see, the mirror in this picture had much more scalloped edges than your mirror. I would also like to take a picture of it. With a photo and my sketching, I am hoping to research in more detail."

Phillip cut in, "By the way, my father finally had a conversation with his European seller of the mirror's shipment. There is no record whatsoever of a mirror in the cargo or manifesto. The seller did not have any record of a mirror in the purchase agreement."

"I don't understand." I looked over at Joe not knowing what to think.

Joe suggested, "Is it possible the mirror was left on the vessel from a previous shipment?"

"It is unlikely as the ships are emptied and cleaned out prior to each voyage but my dad is contacting the shipping company to investigate if anyone is missing a piece." Phillip seemed apprehensive as his eyes kept darting toward the hall.

"Are you OK?" I asked him. "Can I get you anything else to drink?"

"I just can't forget that shock I received from the mirror when I tried to remove it!"

"Well, let me tell you all about my experience last night. Joe, I haven't even told you this yet. Maybe we need something stronger to drink. After all, it's after noon."

There was a nervous round of snickering among us. Joe suggested he could make all of us a Bloody Mary and go out on the back deck to absorb my most recent encounter. Everyone agreed.

Chapter Nine

The Bloody Marys lightened our mood, and in Phillip's case, his tongue.

"It is a strange phenomenon we have going on in this house," Joe mentioned. He snickered as he told them I was afraid of falling asleep because of the "ghost in the mirror." Joe had not yet seen the ghost. He had experienced the sounds of the mirror, but he remained skeptical of any supernatural being.

"I wouldn't be so quick to dispel that theory," Phillip replied cautiously.

"Come on, you aren't really going to tell me you believe in ghosts?"

Phillip took a long drink finishing his Bloody Mary. "Here's the thing, Joe. I am no longer sure. Anna, do you remember when I first met you I asked how well you knew my dad?"

I nodded, wondering where he was going with this.

"Turns out my dad claims he has had more than one encounter with the beyond. These encounters have all been in more recent years through his procurement of articles in the Stillwater Antiques Shop. I never believed him. It started about five years ago, and I figured it was the loneliness of an old man who had lost his wife. Then, last year, while he was extremely busy with two incoming shipments, I came into the Stillwater shop to help. Dad was in the back while I sat up front logging in articles. I was sitting next to a display of Roaring 20's memorabilia when I clearly heard a young woman's voice singing, 'Someone to Watch Over Me.' Assuming a radio had been turned on, I hummed to the tune. After a while, I realized the song was being played over and over. I got up from the desk and walked around to see if I could find the source of the music. Maybe an old record was being played. As I turned the corner of the Roaring 20's display, the music abruptly stopped. An art light was shining on a beautiful framed picture of a young, attractive blonde-haired woman. At the bottom of the frame was an inscribed brass plate that read, 'Mitzi Lewis at the Four Deuces, Chicago, 1926.'"

He continued recalling their conversation. "Just then my father came out. He saw me staring at the picture. 'Is Mitzi singing for you?' he asked with a smirk on his face. 'Dad, did you hear someone singing?' I asked. 'That's Mitzi. She usually sings 'Someone to Watch Over Me.'"

"I stood there gawking at my father, raising my voice at him, accusing him of playing a trick on me."

"He then explained, 'Son, it is not a trick. I know you don't believe in ghosts, but let me tell you about Mitzi. Mitzi was a young singer at a Speakeasy, 'The Four Deuces', over on the south side of Chicago. It was during the mid to late 1920's when gangsters like John Dillinger and Al Capone, crime bosses in Chicago, frequented such places. Capone often requested the Gershwin tune, 'Someone to Watch Over Me,' and he would tell Mitzi she could belt it out better than Gertrude Lawrence. Gertrude Lawrence was the British star of the musical, 'Oh, Kay!', where this song was featured in the 1920's.'"

"I asked him, 'Dad, how do you know all this?'"

"He said, 'Mitzi's relatives moved here from Chicago. They decided to put some of her memorabilia on consignment at the store. It was rumored Mitzi was a 'special friend' of Capone's. Unfortunately, with the violence generated by organized crime during those Prohibition Years, Mitzi was shot in the crossfire and died in 1926.'"

"I stood there looking at Dad as he told me Mitzi often sings to him."

When Phillip was done with his story, we silently sat there, each in our own thoughts.

Phillip continued, "That night, when I got back to my house, I poured myself a Bourbon and Coke, trying to decide if I believed Dad. My mother's voice clearly spoke to me, 'Phil, don't be so hard on your dad. You will not understand until it is too late. Accept there are forces and powers in the afterlife. Some of us choose not to use them, others need resolution in their past lives.'"

No one at the table said a word.

Phillip then spoke, "So, Joe, you ask if I believe, I guess I do."

Chapter Ten

The following day, after an uninterrupted night of sleep, I met Lexi and Donna for lunch at the local Applebee's restaurant. I had not yet told them about my dream or encounters with the mirror. They were excited to know any details that transpired with Phillip and Mark's research. Even "Doubting Donna" was curious. . . maybe a little less skeptical after the shock she received from the mirror.

"Well, it's only been a few days, and it all takes time. I want to tell you the latest, but you may think I'm losing my mind!"

Lexi was first to speak up and tell me she absolutely would not think that.

Donna's response was, "Just tells us. You know I will have no problem letting you know if I think you're going nuts."

I relayed both my nightmare and the apparition I had seen in the mirror. After much silence, Lexi gave her opinion,

"We all know there is something or some power that possesses that mirror. Think of the shock it gave Donna and now Phillip. Maybe it's a ghost from years past trying to get in contact with you?"

Donna shook her head and surprisingly voiced an unusual opinion, "You two know I have never believed in any of this hocus pocus, but I am at a loss of understanding. If it is a ghost, which I haven't believed in, do you think it is trying to take over your body? Maybe re-live through you?"

Lexi impatiently interrupted, "What about the baby? And what about Anna's dream and the blood?"

"Shhh, I don't want anyone else to hear us," I tried to calm Lexi down as I turned my head looking at the other tables.

"Sorry," Lexi whispered, "But, Anna, aren't you afraid to be in that house with the mirror? What if this woman takes over your body, possessing you?"

Donna let out a nervous giggle. I simply sat there, thought about it, and nodded.

"Yes, I am somewhat afraid. I don't want to fall asleep for fear of this person in the mirror but I did sleep well last night. I don't know. Phillip and Mark promised to work on their research right away, and I can't remove the mirror so what can I do? I don't understand why Joe doesn't hear or see this woman when I do?"

Lexi responded, "It is obvious she is drawn to you for some reason. From the beginning, why did you need to have this mirror? You never bought an antique before. I think you need to do some research on yourself too!"

"What do you mean, Lexi?"

"I mean you were an only child, and nowadays anyone can get their DNA analyzed. How much do you know about your ancestors?"

Donna jumped in, "You know, I think that's a great idea! We could find out if your past and your relatives' pasts trace back to whatever and wherever Phillip and Mark find that mirror comes from."

"I doubt that they will be able to find out who it belonged to, but I think I'll do it. As you know, my parents and grandparents have all passed so I don't have anyone that could enlighten me on my family's history, or if there was a family secret I didn't know about. I can sign up on Ancestry.com. It's worth a shot."

Once home, I took a glimpse of the mirror. All was quiet. It was something I now did each time I left, entered, or passed by it. Then I went into the office. We turned our daughter Joanna's bedroom into our office. We have a small house but never felt the need to get a larger one. Our only child, Joanna, named after both Joe and I, was now married and living out east in Willow Grove, Pennsylvania, where her husband, Tom, dabbles at being an artist. Willow Grove is a small quaint, artsy town. He also has a fulltime job as a graphic artist. Joanna is a nurse in the newborn wing of the hospital. They have been married two years now, and Joe and I are praying they have a child soon. Both of them are in their early thirties, so they need to get busy!

I signed onto the computer. Once I found the Ancestry.com site, I decided to join for three months simply to see what I could find out. They offered a DNA test for only $69.95 ($30 off the regular price) when you join. I went for it. Once I joined, I proceeded to enter my basic information to develop a family tree. After typing in my parents' life details and for my grandparents as much information as I could recall, I was stunned when a green leaf suddenly popped up by my name. I read the information about the green leaf and it indicated a "hint" of some kind. It could be a close or extremely distant relative. I clicked on the leaf, and it led me to a name of a possible very distant cousin in England, Nathaniel St. Martin. I had never heard of this person. I would wait until the DNA analysis came back as I didn't want to waste a lot of time checking out "possible very distant cousins." Then a box popped up from Ancestry.com alerting me that I could contact any relatives, but it would only be through Ancestry. In other words, I could draft a message inquiring about any relationship, and Ancestry.com would contact that person. If that person had any details and agreed to communicate with me, they would email me back directly. What the heck! I knew it took several weeks to get the DNA results back, so I sent a message to Nathaniel St. Martin. I explained I was new to this process and his name popped up. I asked if he knew of any possible connection within our families.

Chapter Eleven

There was a chill in the air, so I planned on making chicken soup and dumplings for dinner. Joe should be home by 6:00 pm and it was now almost 4:00 pm, so I had plenty of time. I had to pass by the mirror in the hallway. It started rippling, slowly at first, then more rapidly. I was drawn to it again. I felt like it was calling to me. I sat on the floor only about a foot from the mirror. It continued rippling but not making much noise.

"Who are you and what do you want?" I asked it, surprisingly not yelling, but in a calm voice.

Her image appeared. Once again, it was the woman dressed as I was in my dream. Tears streamed down her cheeks.

"You must find her!" She was pleading with me.

"Who am I supposed to find?" I couldn't believe I was having a conversation with this apparition, and I was remaining composed. After all, I didn't know if it was a spiritual soul or a demon I was communicating with. However, with the devastation and hurt that was etched in her face, I could not refuse this young woman.

"They took my daughter from me. Please find her. Please find the link."

I didn't know what that really meant. "What is your name?"

Her image began to fade. I begged her to tell me her name. Just before the mirror went silent and her image disappeared, I heard her whisper, "My name is Annabelle."

Wow! I sat silently on the hall floor for several minutes trying to understand what had just transpired. I had spoken with a dead person. She had to be dead as she was dressed like she had lived in the 1800's. And how was I to find her daughter? Her daughter would also be long dead. I decided to call Henry at his Stillwater Antiques Shop. Chicken soup and dumplings would have to wait for another day. We could order in. Fortunately, Henry was still at work. I started drilling Henry with questions, question after question, not giving him time to answer. I was nervous, I was scared, I was thinking, maybe I was going mad! I knew I was talking too fast!

Henry cut me off, "Anna, please calm down. You are not going mad. I spoke with Phillip about an hour ago. He is coming down here tomorrow to help out. I suggested I come back with him to the cities. I would like to visit you and discuss the mirror and its history. Would that be OK?"

"Yes, yes, of course! I'm sorry but I don't know what is going on, and I spoke with her just now!"

"You spoke with who?" Henry asked.

"The woman in the mirror. Then she disappeared. But her name is Annabelle! Isn't that funny, her name is Annabelle and my name's Anna."

"Anna, I wouldn't tell too many people about this until we get some answers. I will see you day after tomorrow about noon. Try to remain unruffled and get some sleep."

Ending the conversation with Henry, tiredness enveloped me. I decided to take a nap on the living room sofa. Covering myself with the faded patchwork crocheted afghan my Great-grandma Margaret made for my mother long ago, I was overcome with peace and stillness. This afghan had been handed down to me. I never met my Great-grandmother Margaret as she died before I was born. She lived in Sweden. Her only child was Edward Smith, my grandfather, who came to America in the late 1800's.

The next thing I knew Joe was waking me up. It was almost 7:00 pm. He let me sleep as he knew I must be tired.

"Are you OK, honey?" he asked while touching my forehead with the palm of his hand. "You don't seem to have a fever."

"I'm OK but you need to hear what happened to me today."

"Anna, I am getting concerned about you. Maybe you need to talk with a professional about these visions."

"You mean like a 'shrink'? No, Joe, I simply need answers."

Joe had a troubled look on his face but remained silent. I got up from the couch and as I was folding up my Great-grandmother's afghan, a sudden thought struck me. "My Great Grandmother was from Sweden yet no one in our family, as far back as I can remember, was blonde or seemed to have any Swedish traits or memorabilia from Sweden?" My Grandfather, Margaret's only child, left Sweden in the late 1890's to make a life in America. He had a friend in America who worked the railroads. At that time, the railroads renewed its expansion, and my Grandfather Edward made a successful living in that business. He met my Grandmother, and the rest is history…but who's history? Another reason for the DNA test. I was becoming anxious to see those results.

Chapter Twelve

I told Joe I wanted him home with me when Henry and his son Phillip came by. Joe was getting upset about this entire ordeal. I knew he had doubts about the validity of everyone who was getting involved in our mystery. Joe still thought there was a scientific explanation. He just didn't know how or who could prove it or explain it. This morning we had an argument. We didn't argue much but this one was a bad one and hurtful.

We were sitting at the kitchen table having coffee when Joe started the conversation, "So, tomorrow we are having another visit from the opportunists."

I was hurt and felt Joe had no trust in my judgement. "Joe, I want you to meet Henry. You will see what a kind man he is. They are not opportunists, they aren't even charging me anything for all the work they are doing."

"And what exactly are they doing, Anna? Where is your letter they took? How do you know they aren't making a copy of it and will keep or sell the original? I don't want you being used for their benefit."

"Joe, it's only been a few days. An analysis takes time. Have some faith in me, for God's sake! You haven't been here to see what happens with that mirror. I can't explain why you don't see Annabelle when she appears!"

"Oh, my God! Anna, listen to yourself! She has a name now, a name like yours? This is crazy! That's it! I'm calling Joanna and telling her what is going on here."

"Joe, why would you bother our daughter with this. Just leave it alone until we get some answers. I'm begging you! I am not crazy!" I broke down, crying.

"Anna, the only reason I would call Joanna is she seems to be able to reach you. You two have a connection. You always said you and Joanna could tell each other anything and everything."

"Stop it, Joe! I'm not a child. I'm asking you to be here when Henry and his son come over tomorrow. Just listen to what they have to say!" I was angry — angry enough to stop crying. I could feel the sternness in my glare toward my husband.

"OK, Anna, you win, for now." Joe refilled his coffee cup and went out to the garage. He often spent time out there tinkering, especially when he wanted to mull things over.

I sat in the kitchen thinking how I almost called Joanna yesterday myself. She wouldn't think I was crazy, but now Joe had filled my head with some doubts.

It's funny how coincidences happen. Many people think there are no such things as coincidences. Maybe then it could be ESP or just a strong bond. As I sat there assessing my mental health and my disappointment in Joe, my phone rang. It was Joanna! I was both thrilled and suspicious.

"Did your father contact you to call me?" I questioned.

"No, Mom, why? What's wrong?"

"Just a disagreement. A difference of opinion. No big deal," I tried to downplay my skepticism. "I'm so happy to hear from you, Joanna. How are you and Tom doing?"

"Actually, Mom, we are fantastic! In fact, the reason for my call is we are planning to come out to visit you and Dad next week. Will you be in town?"

Rubbing the back of my neck, I felt sudden palpitations of my heart.

"Mom, did you hear me?"

"Honey, I'm sorry I just had a tickle in my throat," I responded letting out a nervous cough. "Of course, we would love to see you and Tom. Are you taking a vacation? You two work so hard, I can't imagine wanting to spend your time off with your old mom and dad."

"Don't be silly, Mom! Yes, we have both been extremely busy and want to talk to you and Dad about a change we are thinking of making."

"Well, then, by all means. We will be excited to see you, and I promise to make your favorite dish, Chicken Piccata, and your favorite dessert, Chocolate Marshmallow Pie."

"Yummy! I can taste it now!"

"Joanna, be sure to call back and give me the details of your flight so we can pick you up at the airport. I hope you and Tom don't mind sleeping on the sleeper sofa in the office."

"Of course not, but we can also check into a hotel."

As much as I thought that might be a good idea, I didn't want them to do that. "No way will you be spending money for a hotel when we are both retired and have room here. Now, do you want to talk with your dad?"

"I better get back to work. I called to be sure you would be home next week. Give my love to Dad, and I'll call you as soon as I've made our reservations."

"OK Honey, love you!"

"Love you too, Mom."

I stared at my phone after the call ended. "Oh, boy," I thought, "now what do I do about the mirror?" It can't be removed. Maybe when Henry and Phillip come over tomorrow they will have some idea what to do. More than that, I was curious about what change Joanna and Tom were contemplating. She sure sounded happy. I knew Tom loved living out East with the artistic culture, but I also knew Joanna missed home. Maybe a job promotion and another move closer to home? Joanna would be able to get a nursing job anywhere.

I walked to the garage to inform Joe about our impending houseguests. I wanted to see his reaction and then maybe I could tell if he instigated this spur of the moment visit.

Joe seemed genuinely surprised when I told him. He wanted to know the reason for their visit. I simply relayed to him what Joanna had told me.

"Do you think she's pregnant?" Joe asked with a grin on his face.

"You know, Joe, I can't believe I didn't even think of that! Hmm, maybe. We will know soon enough as they will be here next week."

We both expressed a warm, hopeful smile toward each other. Just like that, our argument was forgotten as our thoughts drifted toward a possible grandchild.

Chapter Thirteen

The following morning both Lexi and Donna called wanting to know what the latest was in the mirror investigation. Yes, I had more to tell them and promised the three of us would get together tomorrow as I expected Henry and Phillip here later today. They asked if I received a response back from Nathaniel St. Martin, my "possible" distant cousin. I had not. Donna wanted to see the mirror again and coaxed Lexi into setting aside her fear to also come into the house to see it. They would come over tomorrow afternoon.

Another night and no activity from the hallway where the mirror remained. Earlier this morning I went to the local bakery and picked up a coffee cake and some scones. I was too preoccupied to concentrate on baking and figured the bakery items would be suitable for late morning or early afternoon when I expected Henry and Phillip would arrive. I mixed up a pitcher of Crystal Light Iced Tea and put on a fresh pot of coffee.

It was 1:00 when they arrived. After a bit of small talk, I suggested we go into the dining room where there would be plenty of table space. Phillip carried a large briefcase this time, so I assumed he had papers to show and explain to me. Joe was silent, probably still speculating if these two were "opportunists". I carried in a tray of the bakery items and paper napkins. I asked Joe to help with the drinks. Henry and Phillip used that time to look once again at the mirror.

As we sat down at the dining room table, Phillip asked, "Any recent activity? Dad told me you communicated with a vision?"

I glanced at Joe. He was shaking his head. I knew what I had seen, and I wanted answers no matter how crazy it sounded. "Yes, I did. She even told me her name."

Phillip raised his eyebrows and turned to his dad.

Henry had a somber look on his face but said, "I believe you, Anna. As Phillip has told you, I have had the occasion to see and hear from those who have long ago passed. Joe, I know this is difficult to believe, but please try to remain open and nonjudgmental until you hear us out."

Joe sat at the table with his chin in his hand. He still had somewhat of a smirk on his face. "OK, I will try my best. Please proceed."

Phillip pulled folders out of his briefcase. The first one contained the poem, in a plastic cover. There were additional papers about a quarter of an inch thick.

"First of all, Anna and Joe, here is your original poem. Along with it I am giving you a signed notarized certificate of authenticity."

I questioned Phillip, "How did you get this back so fast?"

"I pulled some strings. I've got friends who substantiate antique documents. I have provided you, in this folder, copies of all the tests made on your document. Your document is an original. We do validate this document is from the year 1837 or there abouts. The ink, script, and paper have all been proven legitimate. Joe, you and Anna can study these papers and you will see the different processes we went through to determine this. Any questions you have on the analysis, please let us know. We had three different sources inspect the documents. Their signatures are at the bottom of the pages. The only step we could not verify is the exact place of origin. Based on the script, wording in the poem, and ink type, we are all in agreement it originated in France or England. We just can't exactly pinpoint which."

I nodded, indicating to Phillip I understood.

Phillip then asked, "Anna, you told me you knew the name in the vision you had. Would you please tell us about that?"

"Sure, it was a few nights ago. She was begging me again to find her daughter. Before she faded away I asked her name. She whispered, 'Annabelle'."

Henry uttered, "That is an old name. Anna, please think hard if there was anything else she could have said."

Joe loudly remarked, "Is this the Twilight Zone? Do you all believe this nonsense! OK, I will concur the poem is legit. I would like to know how much money Anna can get for it. I don't want to hear your far-fetched theories of 'ghosts from the past'."

Before anyone could respond to Joe, the whirring noise started. We all stood up quickly and headed for the hallway. Henry stopped everyone. "Wait, let us all stay back here, except for Anna. This spirit seems to have bonded with Anna for some reason, and it may not appear with all of us. Anna, try to communicate with her again and ask questions of where she is so we can better identify her. We will listen and remain quiet."

I nodded and walked down the hallway toward the mirror. Once again it started rippling. Her image started to come through but then faded back. I decided to call out to her. "Annabelle, can you hear me? Annabelle, please talk to me. I want to help you."

Her image appeared. "Can you find my baby?"

I heard gasping behind me — probably Joe, the nonbeliever.

"Annabelle, where are you? Where do you live?"

"I am no longer here, but you must find the link, find my baby!"

"Annabelle, I promise, but I need help. I don't know where to start. Where are you from? Where were you when your baby was born?"

Annabelle's voice was trembling, and she could not complete an entire sentence. Only certain words came out, "I was…the home…baby gone." She was weeping now.

I wanted to get more information before her image faded away. I never knew when she would make an appearance. "Annabelle, do you know who took your baby?"

"On floor, bleeding...friend, Emma, Emma Brown…. daughter gone. Find link."

The vision vanished.

After a few seconds, I turned to go back into the dining room. Joe was sitting at the table with a terrified expression on his face. Phillip and Henry just stood there, I guess, taking it all in. Myself, I was no longer afraid of Annabelle. Although her daughter would have died long ago, I wanted to help her.

As I sat back down at the table, Joe sheepishly looked up at me. "My God, Anna, how can you ever forgive me? I would not have believed any of this if I had not witnessed it. We have to get that mirror out of our house!"

"Joe, I am no longer fearful of the mirror. I want to help Annabelle."

After several moments of silence, Phillip spoke, "Anna, that conversation was more helpful than you may realize. We now know that Annabelle was in England in 1837, at some kind of a Home. We also have the name of Emma Brown, the last person Annabelle saw with her baby. We can all put our heads together and work on finding any possible connections."

"Phillip, I would like to do that, but 'Brown' is such a common name. I wouldn't know where to start."

Henry cut in with an idea. "You know, Annabelle said to 'Find the Link'.

"Yes, she said that to me the other day also."

"Is it possible, Anna, that there is some connection here? Maybe she appeared to you because you are related? Do you have a family tree, or have you or anyone in your family traced your roots?"

"I just started doing that! I sent in my DNA, but it will take several weeks to get my results. I did, however, get a mention from Ancestery.com that I have a possible distant cousin in England. I sent a message asking if he had any information as to if we were related and how. So far I haven't heard back."

"That is interesting," Henry surmised. "You continue to work on that, and we can search for Emma Brown from England."

I glanced at Joe who looked like he was in shock. "Honey, are you OK?"

"I don't know what to say! I've never believed in spirits or anything like that."

Henry focused his words on Joe. "I was once a nonbeliever. Through the years, I have experienced sounds and visions that could not be explained. I researched the possibilities and did a hell of a lot of reading on the subject. Once I accepted what I could not explain, I became aware that most spirits do not have evil intensions.

They appear to us because of unfinished business on earth — maybe to connect us to something we are totally unaware of or just to tell us their story. When this is accomplished, they disappear."

Joe listened intently but remained silent. Henry continued, "I would, however, be extremely careful about divulging this information to many people. You don't want a media frenzy at your front door."

"I'm not saying anything to anyone," Joe spouted. "I don't want people to think we're crazy!"

I asked Henry and Phillip about my friends and family. "Donna and Lexi already know about the mirror. They were with me when I bought it, and they were here when the rippling started. Donna got a shock from the mirror. Also, our daughter and her husband are coming here next week. They will be staying here with us. What do we tell them? What if the mirror reacts during their visit?"

"That could be a problem." Henry looked at Phillip.

"I would suggest," Phillip replied, "to not tell your friends too much more, unless you absolutely know they will not tell others. Things like this travel fast and get blown out of proportion."

Joe interrupted, "Excuse me, but how more 'blown out of proportion' can this get?"

"I'm just trying to protect you from a media overload." Phillip was trying to calm Joe down. "If you feel you can trust them without being ridiculed, I have no problem with you telling them. As for your daughter, I am sure you know what would be best. You wouldn't want her freaking out in the middle of the night if she heard noises from the mirror. So, I believe you should confide in her but maybe for now, just about the strange noises."

Chapter Fourteen

Joe and I didn't have much to say that evening after Henry and Phillip left. I felt it was a combination of fear of the unknown, not knowing what to do about the mirror, and simply accepting something that our scientific, realistic minds never accepted before. I suggested the two of us go out for a nice dinner. Joe wasn't sure we should leave the house.

"Joe, we can't be held prisoner in our own home from something we don't understand. It would do us good to get out. Please. Besides, we need to decide if and what we are going to tell Joanna and Tom. They'll be here in three days."

Joe agreed. We drove to our local Chinese restaurant. We had eggrolls for an appetizer with a cup of Won Ton soup. Joe ordered beef with snow pea pods for his entrée, and I had my all-time favorite, shrimp with vegetables. Of course, after the appetizers and soup, we realized we definitely did not need an entrée. Nevertheless, we picked at our food while we discussed how to approach Joanna and Tom in a rational way. In the end, we decided to sit them down and show them the documents from Henry and Phillip. We would tell them all about how we found the poem, the strange noises we heard from the mirror, and after hanging the mirror on our wall, trying to remove it resulted in a shock. Joe did not want me mentioning any presence or conversation I had — no mention of Annabelle at all. I didn't know if that was the way to go as I felt we should tell them everything, however, I was finally getting belief and support from Joe, so I hesitantly agreed. We would only pray that Annabelle would choose not to appear during their stay. We packed up our leftovers (enough for at least two nights) and drove home in silence, each contemplating how our lives had been turned upside down by the simple purchase of a mirror.

The next few nights were busy with getting the guest room ready for the kids. The mirror remained silent during this time. I was thankful, being busy preparing Joanna's favorite meals. I did take time out to call my girlfriends asking them not to call or come over while the kids were here. I explained I did not want Joanna and Tom to know all the details, not just yet. I had not received any reply from Nathaniel St. Martin in England.

The weather was turning colder, and we had our first frost of the season. In the morning we drove to the airport to pick up Joanna and Tom. Both Joe and I were nervous fearing the mirror would not remain quiet as it had the last few nights. We thought it would be a good idea to be out of the house most of the time the kids were here, even though I had cooked up a storm.

Once their flight landed, Joanna called to tell us to meet them at what baggage door. Joe stayed in the car while I ran in to greet them. Joanna squealed with delight when she spotted me at the baggage claim. It was so good to see her. As worried as I was with her living out East, it must have done some good as she radiated. My daughter was a beautiful young woman and her husband was not bad either. Tom had all their luggage in tow, and we went to meet Joe. Our trip back to the house was non-stop chit chat.

I couldn't wait until we arrived home, so I turned around in the front seat and looked my daughter in the eye, "Joanna, we are too excited as to what news you have. I need to know now. Are you pregnant?"

Both Tom and Joanna burst out laughing while Joe commented, "My wife, the subtle one!"

"No, Mom, I am not pregnant, but we are thinking about starting a family. That isn't our news. Let's get settled at the house, and we will tell you, so you won't have to wait much longer."

We arrived home in less than a half hour, and I was nervous about the mirror. I wished now that I had not put the mirror in the hallway where the bedrooms were. There was nothing I could do about it now and silently prayed to God that all would remain quiet. The kids did not have much luggage as they were only staying for a long weekend.

Once unpacked, Joanna spotted the mirror. "Mother, is that a new piece?"

"Oh, it's just a little mirror I picked up on my annual shopping trip with Lexi and Donna. Let's go into the kitchen and sit while I get you a snack." I was trying my best to steer her away from the hallway.

As we sat at the kitchen table, Joanna seemed interested in knowing more about the mirror. "Mom, it's not like you to purchase antique pieces."

Joanna, growing up in the midst of my friendship with Donna and Lexi, knew them well and was aware of our annual treks. She knew how I often commented "antiques were just someone else's junk".

I tried to downplay my purchase and change the subject but Joe spoke up about the hidden letter. We had agreed to tell them the basics of the purchase but not about the apparitions and dreams I had.

"Oh my God, Mom, that is so awesome! Can we see the letter?"

Hesitantly, I showed them the letter, asking not to remove it from the plastic sheath.

Tom asked, "Do you know anything about it, like it's origin?"

"Yes, I have a friend in Stillwater who has authenticated it. Its origin is either England or France, and the year of the letter, 1837, is correct."

"What are you going to do with it?" Tom asked.

"I'm not sure. We just found it so we need time to consider our options."

Tom looked at Joanna and winked at her. "This is kind of ironic, but it leads us into our news."

Joe now sat down at the table. We were both eager to hear the news.

Joanna began, "Mom and Dad, as you know, in addition to Tom's full-time job as a graphic artist, he creates oil and watercolor paintings and does some clay work on his own. Twice a year in Willow Grove there is an art fair that Tom participates in. He has done consignment work for a regular customer, Jonathan. Recently, Jon moved back to England where he teaches at The University of Art, London. The school carries a reputation of being a world-leading University in art, design, and communication. The educators do a rotation of six major art schools in the United Kingdom."

My eyes darted back and forth between Tom and Joanna. Joe jumped in, "And?"

Tom took over, "Jon has become a friend to us as well as a good customer. He likes my work. He has asked if I would consider being a guest speaker and demonstrating and creating some art pieces on a tour of the six schools. It would only take a few months to complete the rotation, of which he would pay me quite well. Joanna and I are thinking of taking a leave of absence from our jobs for six months to visit Europe. I'm asking my parents if they would consider coming out sometime after my rotation is complete, and we would like the two of you to visit also. Jon told me he would find a place big enough to accommodate any visitors I would like. Would you please consider it?"

Joanna interjected, "And then, after we return home, we plan on starting a family."

Joe looked at me and said, "I don't like to fly, but if I can't see my baby girl for six months, by God, I'm going to Europe!"

Our laughter was interrupted by a noise coming from the hallway.

Chapter Fifteen

The noise startled all of us. Joe and I locked eyes while Joanna requested to know what the noise was.

At first, Joe and I didn't say anything but then Tom uttered, "You two look like you've seen, or in this case, heard, a ghost!"

The mirror continued with its sound, and before we could stop them, Joanna and Tom raced into the hallway in the direction of the noise. We followed them. The mirror was rippling again! Oh, God, I prayed Annabelle would not make an appearance. Once all four of us stood there gawking at the mirror, it stopped.

"Mother, your mirror. Whatever is that?" Joanna exclaimed.

Tom was curious and stepped toward the mirror. I was nervous and afraid. I yelled, too quick and loud, "Tom, don't touch that!"

Both Tom and Joanna looked at me like I had gone crazy.

Joe came to the rescue, "Let's sit down in the living room, and we will explain as best we can."

Once settled, Joe took the lead, careful not to mention Annabelle or the apparitions, as had been our agreement. In the end, we simply told them we had Henry, Phillip, and Mark studying the situation and probing all possibilities. I apologized to Tom saying I did not mean to yell at him, but the mirror was capable of giving him a shock that would knock him on his fanny.

Rubbing his right eyebrow like he had a nervous twitch, Tom stated with some disbelief, "There has to be a scientific explanation. I'm just an artist with no electrical or physics education, but it has to be an issue of magnetic energy after the mirror was mounted on the wall."

"We just don't know," I hopelessly declared. "The whole situation has put us on edge, and I'm having strange dreams. It's like the sounds come from the mirror at no particular time, and I wish it would stop!" I was getting too worked up. Joe put his arm around me but comfort didn't come. I started to cry.

Joanna came over and sat on the other side of me. "Mom, I'm so sorry you are going through this, both of you. What can we do to help?"

I was so close to divulging all. To tell her about Annabelle but I knew they might question my sanity. I started to compose myself. "There is nothing you can do. We have the best people we know to work on it. I didn't want to burden you with this during your short stay."

"It's OK, Mom. I only wish I knew what to do."

I then saw the look my daughter gave her dad. The look of "We'll talk later." Well, FLASH NEWS to Joanna, as Joe had now witnessed what I had.

"OK, enough of this talk. We will figure it out. Anna just needs to get some improved sleep." Joe was trying his hardest to get things back on a more normal focus. "I have an idea. We have a new deli that opened up. Let's go there for lunch. I'm sure it's not as good as your delis out East, but it'll pass."

We all agreed. I freshened up, removing the tear stains from my eyes and applied a rose-toned lipstick, feeling now passable for going out in public. We headed out to the car. Stopping at the door and giving the excuse I better use the bathroom first, I told them to go out to the car, and I would be right out.

Once I knew the three of them were situated inside the car, I stood before the mirror, begging, "Please, Annabelle, don't make an appearance until the children are gone. I promise I will help you. I will find your link, but please, wait a few days."

I rushed out to the car, and we were on our way. I knew Joanna had already noted her concerns to Joe about me, and hopefully he had calmed her fears.

Our lunch at the deli was almost as good as those out East. We munched on Rueben sandwiches and French Dips, but I advised everyone to go easy at lunch as Chicken Piccata and Chocolate Marshmallow Pie was for dinner. Both Joanna and I left with a doggie bag, but Joe and Tom happily devoured their meals. We were too stuffed to do much more so we headed back to the house. Joanna said a nap would do her good, and I had to agree. After the emotional start of the day, it sounded good to me too.

I woke after a good hour of napping. Joanna's nap was what she referred to as 'her usual 30-minute power nap.' Working long hours and different shifts at the hospital, she often took advantage of power nap opportunities.

"Mom, how about you and I go get a massage tomorrow. Maybe it will help you relax."

Sensing her concern for me, I agreed, but told her she need not worry, I would be fine. I could talk to Joe tonight after we went to bed as it was evident they had been discussing my 'well-being'.

It was fun to see how much my daughter still loved my cooking. We all enjoyed Chianti wine with our Italian dinner and discussed Tom and Joanna's upcoming trip and when would be the best time to cross the ocean and visit them. I was getting excited. There was so much to get done before we left. Passports had to be obtained, depending upon the time of year and the weather, I would definitely have to buy some new clothes, and walking shoes. I had to have comfortable walking shoes. Maybe it was the wine, but for the first time since I brought that mirror into our home, I did not think about it, I simply enjoyed our family. I believed it would be good for Joe and I to get away. We hadn't been on a trip for some time and we had never been to Europe.

That night, once we were settled in bed, I asked Joe if the children were questioning my sanity.

"No, Anna. They are just concerned. I set them straight. I don't know, maybe they think we are both going insane now as I told them again I heard everything you did."

I silently said a prayer of thanks for Annabelle's lack of appearance that night.

Chapter Sixteen

Joanna and Tom's visit was too short. However, I was somewhat relieved when they left. I could not truly relax the entire time they were here, worried about the mirror and Annabelle. To our amazement, both the mirror and Annabelle remained silent. I told Joe what I had done before leaving for lunch that day. We contemplated if Annabelle actually heard and understood my request; if there was a presence now in our home that was aware, even if we could not see the spirit. We had succumbed to the belief of spirits. How could we not?

Joanna took the time during our trip to the spa to make me promise to inform her of all the details of the letter and mirror once we had answers. We never mentioned Annabelle to her. At this point, there was no need to.

The day after Tom and Joanna left, I decided to check my email as I had not gotten on my computer their entire visit. It seemed as if my heart jumped up into my throat when an email appeared from Nathaniel St. Martin. He was friendly in his email relaying to me he had no idea how we were related. In fact, he had only recently signed up on Ancestry.com, just as I had. He had questions on his own heritage and to his knowledge, since the recent death of his mother, he had no remaining relatives. He was hopeful when he also received a leaf with my name. Nathaniel asked if it would be acceptable if we correspond directly with each other, outside of Ancestry.com, in order to speed up the process of our investigation. I emailed him back with my approval and suggested we give each other details, as much as we knew, of ourselves and our families. We would work together on this journey and hopefully find the answers we both sought.

My first reply to Nathaniel mentioned all the basic information (my age, Joe's age, and our daughter, Joanna's age). I also included information on those relatives I knew of, explaining that I did not have much to go on, but I could trace my family back to my great grandmother in Sweden. Jokingly, I told him I didn't know where the Swedish part came in as no one in our family had blonde hair. I kept my message brief in hopes he may be able to fill in some of the blanks.

Two days later, Nathaniel responded. Unfortunately, all of his roots began and ended somewhere in England. He was one year older than I was, married to Catherine, and had two grown children — a son, Jonathan, and a daughter, Charlotte. He thought maybe Ancestry.com made a mistake in tying us together with a leaf. I sent back a reply informing him I wanted to see if my DNA testing came back with anything different. It would take a few weeks yet, but I would contact him again if I discovered a link between us. There was that word, "link", just like the ghost of Annabelle mentioned.

I signed off the computer just as I heard the mirror. It had been almost a week since it attempted any kind of communication. Joe was busy in the garage. It was now mid-November, and I wanted him to start getting out the Christmas decorations. Joanna and Tom would not be here for Thanksgiving, as they only left about two weeks ago, but they planned on staying with us during Christmas. Approaching the mirror with some reservation, Annabelle's face appeared.

Her words were disjointed, and I had to listen intently to understand. "Did find link?" she asked.

"I am working on it, Annabelle. I don't know where else to look."

"Find friend, Emma Brown. Held baby up…daughter…she took."

With that, the image evaporated. It seemed like each vision was fainter than the last one, and Annabelle's speech was getting softer each time. I headed out to the garage to let Joe know just as my phone beeped. It was Joanna.

"Hi Mom. How are you doing?"

My daughter was calling me already. Convinced she was concerned about me, I told her, "Honey, I'm doing OK. Really. Please don't be so worried about me."

"I do worry about you, Mom, but that isn't the reason I'm calling. Where is Dad?"

"He's out in the garage, rummaging through Christmas decorations and probably cussing at lights being tangled." We both laughed knowing this was an every-year event.

"Good. Maybe I caught him in time. Would you please call him in from the garage and put your phone on speaker so you both can hear this?"

"Sure, Honey."

Hurrying out to the garage, I could only imagine what Joanna wanted us both to hear. Was the trip off? Maybe they decided to have a baby sooner? I could only speculate.

"Ok, Honey, we are both here, on speaker." I heard Joanna belt out a loud yawn.

"Are we keeping you up?" Joe asked.

"No. I just haven't been sleeping very well. In fact, I haven't slept well since our trip to Minneapolis."

Joe and I both flinched. "Are you having bad dreams, Joanna?" Joe asked with some fear.

"No, not bad dreams, nothing to worry about. Anyway, I have some exciting news, and I hope both of you can join us. We planned on our trip being after the holidays. However, Tom had an awesome idea. His parents are always way too busy with parties during this time, and we thought it would be exciting if we spent Christmas in England! You know, leave early, forget all the hustle and bustle of decorating and cooking. Try out some figgy pudding and have a

'Dickens' type of holiday. We want you two to come with and help us get settled before Tom's six-month tour begins. Tom and I have plenty of vacation stored up so we would have no problem taking that in addition to our already planned leave of absences."

Joe and I didn't know what to say.

"Please Mom and Dad. I'm your only child. What would Christmas be without me?"

"She's right, Joe." I agreed without knowing what Joe was thinking.

"Joanna," Joe began. "We haven't gotten our passports yet. We were going to go apply this week. With the holidays, I can't imagine we could get them soon enough. When are you two planning on leaving?"

"We thought the week before Christmas would give us enough time to settle into the place that Jon is arranging for us. Then we can enjoy the holiday in Merry Old England."

"I would like to avoid untangling the Christmas lights this year. Otherwise, I could simply throw them out and buy new ones. But if you aren't going to be here, I wouldn't feel like decorating." Joe looked dejected.

"Mom, Dad, let me talk with Tom to see if he has a way of speeding up the process of obtaining your passports. I'm wondering if we get Jon involved. Maybe he could possibly push it through, indicating 'for educational purposes'."

Joe cut in, "Are you kidding? I don't think the government would care two cents for that, but I do know there is a way with business travel that it can be expedited. Maybe to pay more money. Ok, you check, and we will go down today to apply, and I'll try to get some information. What do you think, Anna? Want to spend Christmas in Merry Old England if we can get our passports?"

"Yes!" I squealed in delight. "Put those decorations away until next year, Joe. Let's see what we can do!"

Chapter Seventeen

The next several weeks were crazy! We applied for our passports and were relieved to find out there was a way to get an expedited passport in about two to three weeks by paying an additional fee. We could do it! Excitement set in for both of us. I needed to check out the weather this time of year in England to see what I should pack (or buy) to wear. Joe and I didn't make the traditional Thanksgiving dinner. Instead, we went to a brunch that was good but way overpriced. I never understood why brunches did not include the cost of the beverage with the meal. Crazy, the brunch would be advertised for $30 per person, but by the time they added in coffee or mimosa, tax and tip, you could spend up to $50 per person. This must be the way people think once they are retired and on a fixed income — especially when we need to take money out of our savings for the upcoming trip. But that's what our savings was for, and this was an important new experience to spend with our daughter. We would be creating new memories.

Lexi and Donna were happy for us. I told them it had been about a week since I had heard any noises from the mirror. I wondered if it was over, as Annabelle's condition looked so wane and her vision had decreased in appearance. I had been sleeping much better these days without any troublesome dreams. Joe and I did not speak of it during this period of silence.

Henry, Phillip, and Mark kept in touch with me. Henry still could not find any record of the mirror being on the ship. Therefore, he could not provide me with the Antiques Shop's certificate of authenticity but was happy his son and Mark were able to craft one that was valid and notarized. Phillip and Mark continued digging for clues to identify the owner or history of the poem and mirror. So far, they had come up with nothing. Joanna emailed me a few times this past week also inquiring about it. Donna wanted to write about the mirror and the hidden poem to send an article off to a magazine or newspaper. I begged her not to, especially since I had not divulged everything to my friends about Annabelle. I finally convinced Donna that it was my story to write. She wasn't happy but, of course, she never is.

I sat down at my computer to get caught up on emails. My DNA results were in from Ancestry.com! A graph listed percentages showing ethnicity estimates. A pie chart broke down the areas on a map and indicated those percentages. There were small percentages listing Ireland, Scotland, and Germanic Europe with the majority of ethnicity, 62%, designated as England, Wales, and Northwestern Europe. There was no indication of Sweden, where my Great-grandmother Margaret was from. I remembered how I questioned the lack of blonde hair in my family and my Great-grandmother's background. I called out to Joe who was watching television. He came into the office, and I voiced my concern about Great-grandma Margaret.

"Are you sure they didn't make a mistake on that DNA? You even corresponded with that St. Martin guy, and he had no clue how you could possibly be related."

"Maybe, but I wonder. Now that I am a member on this website, I can go back and pull up records like my family's birth, marriage, and death certificates. I have to do this. Maybe this is the link that Annabelle referred to."

"Honey, don't go getting crazy now. We have a big trip to think about. Maybe you should go shopping and get your mind off of this."

A typical male chauvinist remark, I thought, but didn't say anything to him. Joe went back to watch his sports channel. I decided to email Nathaniel St. Martin telling him about my DNA results and letting him know I was coming to England very soon. Having no idea where he resided, compared to where we would be staying, I suggested, if possible, we could meet to discuss our possible related heritage. I would email him again once I knew where we would be staying.

Next, I started filling out the family tree on the web site and searched for family records. I started with my mother and father. My dad's name was Robert Clark. His relatives were easily found and someone in his family had already filled out a family tree.

Nothing questionable there. On my mother's side, I filled in all of her brothers and sisters. Every one of them had already passed. Mom had been the youngest. I listed all five children on the family tree, Edward, Jr., William, James, Emma, and my mother, Elizabeth. I knew my mother had trouble getting pregnant and finally at age thirty, she gave birth to me. Why hadn't we been closer to her siblings? Or their children? They were scattered across America, and we occasionally heard from them with a Christmas card. I remember visiting them from time to time when they were in town or we traveled and stopped by to see them. I was very young and don't recall much. My eye caught the name of Emma. That was the name Annabelle said took her baby. Well, it had to be a coincidence as that was in 1837, one hundred years before my Aunt Emma would have been born.

I searched for my grandparents' information. It was amazing how accessible these records were on the internet. My grandfather, Edward Smith, married Mary Fisher in 1893. My grandfather, Edward, headed to America from Sweden, in 1892 to work on the then booming railroad industry. He had a friend from college in the industry and together they made a small fortune. So, this is where the "Sweden" link came in. There was no marriage record of my Great-grandmother, Margaret, married to Albert Smith. This would then be my grandfather Edward's parents. Like my mother and father, they only had the one child, Edward, born in 1862. I did not know my Great-grandmother Margaret's maiden name. Searching for this, I ran into a dead end. Well, enough for today. I was getting tired. Just then, Joe called to me. He was standing at the mirror as I approached him.

"I tried to see if the mirror would now come off as it has been silent for a while, but I got shocked, and I thought I saw that woman's image but then it went away." Joe was still having such trouble accepting this entire ordeal.

"Honey, why don't you go back in the living room. I need to make dinner but first I want to see if I can communicate with her again."

Before Joe left, he told me I should leave well enough alone. I probably should but I didn't.

"Annabelle, can you hear me?" I was surprised when she suddenly appeared looking clearer then the last time.

"I am always with you, we are only a breath away. In life and death, we are only a breath away. The link, did you find it?" Her speaking was now much stronger than before.

"I'm working on it. Annabelle, can you tell me who the father of your child was?"

"Richard. What happened to Richard?" Annabelle started to fade as I saw tears rolling down her cheeks.

England
PART TWO
Chapter Eighteen

Christmas in England! The streets and shops were decorated like something out of an old Dickens story book. The Brits decorate in red and green like we do in the United States. However, they also use gold as a primary Christmas color. The hangings on the street light posts may not have been as fancy as ours, but the simple swags of holly, ivy, and mistletoe with gold ribbon and white lights provided a feeling of tradition and hope. England decorates with more outside Christmas trees than we do. All around town you will see various trees, often oversized, trimmed with lights, gold ribbon, apples, and oranges. The fruit on the trees are for anyone to enjoy and replenished daily by merchants. Indoor trees are also decorated with fruit and strung with old fashioned popcorn and cranberries.

It was our third day in London. I remember wandering the streets and doing some shopping with a feeling like I had gone back in time. It was a pleasant feeling though, a relaxation time after the hectic flight here. I was not crazy about flying even though we had a direct flight from Minneapolis to England. Knowing my fear of flying, Joanna and Tom thoughtfully drove to Minneapolis so we could all be on the same flight. No matter how prepared I was for a trip, I always packed way too much clothing and toiletries. You never know what the weather will be like or how fancy a dinner place will be, so we were already tired lugging our suitcases around before we checked the baggage. The early morning flight itself was smooth until we started crossing the ocean. The amount and strength of turbulence was so scary I prayed an entire rosary! I wanted to kiss the ground when we arrived at Heathrow but thought better of it after seeing dirty, questionable people loitering about.

Joanna and Tom's friend, Jon, had booked a lovely, spacious, place for them to stay. It wasn't a hotel or flat. It was more of a country house but not in the country. Jon had referred to it as a "European Bungalow" — a house which is only on one floor with no stairs. Some of these bungalows may be joined to another but this one was a stand-alone type. It was fully furnished and had a washer and dryer. A very nice place to stay for their six-month duration.

That first night we were all tired, suffering from jet lag. We spent the time unpacking and napping. After the four of us showered and changed clothes, we headed out in search of a restaurant. The bungalow was about a half-mile from a primary shopping and eating area. Outside was a bit balmy. There was no snow, and it seemed warm enough wearing a light coat to walk. We settled for a small shack-type eating place that advertised they had "The best Fish and Chips in the world". What a disappointment! England's fish and chips are nothing like the ones in America. The fish tasted very fishy and had many white bones in it. In the US we use cod fish, I believe, and there aren't any bones — at least none that are noticeable. The chips were French fries, which was OK, but they tasted like they were fried in the same "fish oil". None of us finished our meals, hoping this was not how most food was here in England. Walking back to the bungalow, we stopped at an ice cream shop in hopes the dessert would remove any residue of fish taste. It worked! There were so many choices. I splurged on a cup of cherry ice cream drizzled with hot chocolate sauce and fresh whipped cream. We planned on venturing out to a grocery store during our first week to stock up the refrigerator, but we would all definitely come back to this shop for more ice cream.

The next evening, we went to a classier restaurant that Jon had suggested. It was Italian and in a building that you had to walk downstairs to get to, like walking into a basement. It was extremely dark, making me wonder what I was actually eating or if anything was crawling around. A good Chianti soothed any fears I had. The food was excellent. I had a meat Ravioli dish, and Joe opted for Lasagna. Joanna and Tom enjoyed the spaghetti and meatballs. Garlic bread was warm and tasty. Refills of the bread were abundantly served, without asking, as was the wine. I felt a little tipsy. The service was outstanding. Two thumbs up for this one. I slept well that night.

On our third day in London, we wandered along Bicester Village in London. It was a quaint area with wooden benches in front of most of the shops so we could rest when needed. Carolers strolled the area wearing old time hats and coats that looked like the ones worn in <u>A Christmas Carol</u>. Their voices added much charm to this already festive area, however, I had to admit when they sang "Silent Night" I felt a little homesick and teary eyed. The next day Jon had arranged for us to see the palace and witness the Changing of the Guard. Then we would need to rest a day or two before Jon flew in from New York to spend some time with us. I planned on calling Nathaniel St. Martin during that time for a meet up. I also needed to talk with Joanna alone. Since we were in England, each night I heard her talking in her sleep. I couldn't make out exactly what she was saying but I did hear reference to a baby and running away. Hopefully she remembered her dreams and would confide in me.

Chapter Nineteen

My belief in "coincidences" was scrupulously tested days later. Did I still believe in coincidences or was there some greater power directing us like puppets on strings, turning and pointing us in the direction we needed to be? Was this God?

My first encounter that made me feel I was having an "out of body" experience was, of course, the mirror and Annabelle. I still had not told Joanna I had spoken with an apparition, let alone tell her the spirit's name. I finally believed Annabelle was truly a spirit reaching out to me, but I did not know why until we were ready to return home from England.

During our few days of rest before Jon would arrive, I spoke with Joanna, worried about her dreams. "Joanna, I've heard you talking in your sleep. Are you worried about anything? The reason I ask is that I have heard you each night you have been here. Is anything wrong?"

"Mom, I'm fine but I have had some strange dreams. Maybe it's thinking about starting a family later, or just being in a different place. I don't know. I've never had a recurring dream before and this one was a doozie. It was so weird. I dreamt that I had given birth, alone, without any help whatsoever. I had this great sense of fear and immediately needed to hide my baby but there was nowhere to hide."

At first, I didn't know what to say. Thoughts of Annabelle flooded my mind, but my main concern was to comfort my daughter.

"Honey, I'm sure being in a strange place has something to do with those dreams. Remember, too, we had all been discussing you and Tom having a child. Sometimes our sub-conscious is having fun with us. Also, don't forget that you have worked in a hospital with new born babies for a long time and have recently given that up for six months. Maybe you're feeling that loss right now."

It was the only thing I could think of quickly and Joanna seemed to accept that, especially about her career at the hospital. She continued to have similar dreams but not every night.

After my talk with Joanna, I quietly told Joe about it that night in our bedroom. I got goosebumps relaying the information. He was quiet as I believe he had learned not to question my improbable accounts.

His only response was, "Anna, it has been a nice few days not worrying about the mirror and Annabelle. Please, let's not create something that isn't there, at least for now. I believe in what you see and think, but I don't want the kids getting upset. Please put this on the back burner for now."

I wasn't angry with Joe but simply had another strange feeling about this. Another coincidence that both Joanna and myself dreamt of babies being taken or hidden?

Then, there was our meeting with Nathaniel St. Martin. Joe and I met Nathaniel and his wife, Catherine, at a Starbuck's coffee shop by Heathrow. They lived a longer distance from our bungalow and wanted to meet close to the airport because their son would be coming home from the states later in the day. Joe and I took a taxi to the coffee shop, which was a little costly. Nathaniel informed us Uber operates in London, so that is how we would get back to the bungalow. I knew Joe wasn't crazy about coming along, but I needed him there for validation in case I found out something worthwhile. I didn't want anyone to think I was crazy. After all, I already spoke to spirits.

We had a friendly visit. Nathaniel still did not know how we could possibly be related but was open to finding out. He apologized for not taking time to do his "due diligence" but promised to help me in any way he could. His wife, Catherine, remembered Nathaniel's mother working on a family tree and tracing ancestral roots.

"It was a passion of hers," Catherine reminisced. "The last several years of her life, she was obsessed with completing it, but I don't think she ever did."

"Would you know where that information would be? I didn't see anything on Ancestry.com." I was probably being over inquisitive.

"Anna, back then there was no 'Ancestry.com'." Catherine smiled, but then, like a lightbulb going off, she remembered something. "Nathaniel, what did we ever do with that old trunk of your mother's? Maybe all her paperwork would be in there."

Nathaniel thought a while and then replied, "I bet it's in our storage locker. You know living here, unlike the states, most of us reside in flats with not a lot of storage room. After my mother passed away, I put most of her things in a storage locker. How long are you staying in England? I will look through my mother's things and let you know before you leave."

It was a ray of hope for me. I told them we would be in England a few more weeks. We settled down then and enjoyed our coffee and scones. Catherine told us how proud she was of her son and so happy he was coming home for a while.

"What does your son do?" Joe asked.

"He teaches at the University, but goes back and forth to the United State often. He's only been gone a short time but plans on staying in England now except for short trips to shows and galleries."

"What subject does your son teach at the University?" I wondered as shows and galleries sounded like Tom's forte.

"He teaches art. First, he tried the New York Wallstreet scene as a stock broker but didn't like the 'atmosphere', if you know what I mean. He found more fulfillment in teaching and studying art, even though the money wasn't as much. He is doing quite well now. This week he is meeting up with a couple from the states. They are from out East and will help Jon with art studies," Catherine explained.

"Wait a minute!" I raised my voice a little too high. "I can't remember. What is your son's name?"

"It's Jonathan." Nathaniel responded, looking bewildered at my emotional state.

"Oh, my God!" I exclaimed. "Our daughter and son-in-law are meeting with their friend Jon for a six-month art teaching assignment. I never heard what Jon's last name was, but could he be the same person?"

Well, Jon turned out to be one and the same. Joe called Tom while we sat at the café and confirmed that his friend Jon's last name was St. Martin. Another coincidence? I felt as though my life was being controlled by an invisible force manipulating the strings of me as the puppet. I couldn't even speak. I sat there mesmerized wondering where this spellbound journey was taking us. Catherine promised she and Nathaniel would go to the storage locker in the next day or two and get back to us.

Chapter Twenty

Joanna and Tom could not believe the person I spoke of meeting on Ancestry.com was the father of their friend and colleague. I guess I never mentioned his name to them. I couldn't sleep wondering how all of the coincidences in our lives were being played out. Neither Joe nor I had thought to bring a computer, but thank goodness, Tom and Joanna had. After all, they couldn't be gone for six months without one, especially with Tom teaching and studying Art. So, whenever I could, I spent time on Joanna's laptop, once again exploring any possibilities of a relationship to the St. Martin's. Could this possibly be the "link" Annabelle had spoken of?

After nights of research, I wasn't any closer to a resolution than when I started. Disappointment and fatigue finally took over, and I slept an entire day and night. My family was concerned but knew I needed the rest. The much-needed sleep did make me feel refreshed, and I was happy to hear that Nathaniel St. Martin had phoned Joe and wanted to meet with us to discuss the findings in their storage locker. They invited us, along with Joanna, Tom, and Jon to their home for dinner. When we finally met Jon, I studied him to see any resemblance to family members, but I could not identify any. He was much taller and thinner than anyone in my family. He was attractive with dark, curly hair and eyes so green in the light they reflected almost like emeralds. He had a Romanesque nose but not overly pronounced. All of us were excited to see how we could possibly be related.

The St. Martin's house was a quaint, modest two-bedroom home. It resembled more of a cottage on the countryside. Nathaniel explained that many homes were destroyed during World War II and replaced with pre-fab houses. This little brick cottage somehow remained standing with minimal damage. I thought it was odd there wasn't much furniture in the home, only an old wooden dining room table and chairs with worn upholstery on the seats. There was a small sofa in the living room. I didn't see any television.

"I thought you lived in a flat. Isn't that what you said when we met for coffee? You had to move your mother's trunk into storage, right?" I was confused.

"We actually do live in a flat, several miles away. Remember I told you that my mother passed away last year? Well, this was her home. It is ours now, and we have been attempting to clean it out. I put many things in storage, including the trunk we spoke of, as we don't want anyone breaking in and stealing something. We plan on moving here in a few months. Our flat is so small I wanted to have dinner here where everyone would be comfortable."

Catherine came out of the kitchen. "I have a nice roast in the oven with Irish potatoes and carrots. I am trying to cook more for Americans, so I hope you like it."

"What can I help you with?" I wanted to hear about what they found in the trunk but knew I had to be polite and offer to help.

"This roast has about an hour to cook. I haven't set the table yet as I thought we could spread out the papers from the trunk and see if we can decipher anything that could be advantageous to your search."

In the corner of the living room I spotted the old trunk. I would call it medium sized, similar to a small coffee table. It did, however, look heavy as it was solid wood with straps of embossed tin covering each side.

"Oh, my goodness," I slapped my hand against my heart. "You brought the entire trunk. Wasn't it heavy?"

Nathaniel smiled and said, "Come on over here and see it. It's old but interesting. It actually has wheels on it although they are in serious need of repair, which we will do, if we decide to keep it."

I walked over to the trunk. Feeling as though I was in the presence of an antique and who knows what it was worth, I gently traced my fingers over the dark wood scroll work, which was partially covered by the embossed tin straps. I could not believe the leather handles were still intact, and they did look like the original handles. The top of the trunk was a dome humpback. There was a latch that would lock the trunk once the top was closed. I did notice a few white, chalky marks surrounding the bottom base. It could have been water marks or just aging. Other than that, it seemed in good shape, and I wondered how old it was.

"Catherine and Nathaniel, this is a real treasure. How old do you think it is?" I was curious and wondered if it had been in their family throughout time.

Catherine reminisced as she spoke. "I remember Nathaniel's mother telling me that this trunk held many secrets throughout the lives of those who had it in their possession. She never elaborated, but she spent much of her later years trying to reach into the past, as her own mother had done, to find family members."

I was puzzled. "Didn't she know who her ancestors were?"

"Apparently her great-grandmother told a story of a missing child. I don't know all of the details, but let's start looking through the papers we pulled out of the trunk as dinner will be ready soon."

Joe and I stared at each other wondering if the missing child could have been Annabelle's, but for now, we remained silent. Nathaniel carried out a manila folder overfilled with papers. All six of us sat down at the table. Catherine, Nathaniel, and I tried to put the jumbled mess into some kind of order. The others simply looked on as there was not much else to do without a television. Besides, they were all curious as to what could possibly be discovered. We each took a stack of papers and tried to sort, but it was nearly impossible. We didn't understand what Nathaniel's mother's method was or what chronological order this mess was in. Digging through my pile, my breath stopped for a moment as I came across a hand-written family tree.

I handed it to Nathaniel so he could interpret who was who. He studied it closely. Trying to decipher his mother's antiquated handwriting, he smiled, remembering older, now deceased family members he had known.

"I have an idea," he uttered. "Anna, you have started a family tree, right?"

I nodded.

"Do you have it with you? If not, could you write down as much as you remember, and we can see if there are any similarities to my family tree?"

I had started one but didn't bring it with me as it was on the computer. "I could get it when we go back to the bungalow as it is on Joanna's computer."

Catherine interrupted telling us the table needed to be cleared for dinner. We could continue after or maybe tomorrow if everyone was tired.

We helped Nathaniel clean up the papers trying to keep them in some kind of order. I walked with him back to the trunk. He put the folder of papers inside the trunk when something glimmered and caught my eye.

"What is that, Nathaniel?"

"Who knows? I haven't yet gone through all of this, but let's see."

He slowly moved some small boxes away from the shiny object and pulled out a mirror. A mirror that was identical to the one in our home! It was cracked but it was the same. I shrieked for Joe. Everyone rushed toward me as I suddenly felt a warm rush throughout my body and toppled to the floor.

Chapter Twenty-One

Once I awoke, I was lying on the sofa with everyone around me looking concerned. "What happened? How did I get on the sofa?" My mind was muddled.

Joanna, looking scared and concerned, held my hand and asked if I remembered fainting. Silent and thinking for a few minutes, the fogginess started clearing from my head.

"Yes, I do remember getting hot, like all the blood was rushing to my head. How long have I been on the sofa?" I know I seemed fretful, but most of all I was embarrassed.

Joe spoke up informing me that both he and Nathaniel picked me up and elevated me to the couch. Nathaniel was getting doctor's contact information for Joe to call when I came to. I could tell Joe was worried as he continually rubbed his face and talked too fast, which he always did in stressful situations. Alarmed and fearing dinner was ruined, to my relief, I had only been out a matter of minutes.

I sat up on the sofa. Everyone's faces seemed like they were gawking at me. Too many eyes glued in my direction.

"Well, I'm hungry. Let's eat." I did my best to be uplifting and calm.

Joe helped me to the table, steering me protectively with his arm across my back. Catherine wondered if trying to figure out these family dynamics had been too much for me. I knew the fainting spell was most likely a slight shock from seeing that mirror. Not yet sure that Joe or Joanna had seen the mirror with all the hubbub surrounding my collapsing on the floor, I remained silent about it.

Dinner was delicious. It was just what I needed, a plentiful, home cooked meal. I stayed away from any additional wine or alcohol. Still not too crazy about most of the food we tried in England, even the groceries we found at the stores had such a sparse selection compared to any back home. So, this dinner was just what the doctor ordered. Because of my brief fainting spell, everyone else decided we should not continue any research that evening. Disappointed, but seeing their concern, I agreed. Nathaniel and I would work on our family trees and meet again to see if there were any similarities. He and Catherine agreed to come to the bungalow day after tomorrow for lunch and compare our information.

On our way home, I knew everyone was concerned about me, but I really did feel fine. I was just tired of guessing what was going on and tired of what seemed to be games being played with my mind and my heart. Most of all, I was sad and tired that I did not know my history. Sometimes I wished I never would have started this search but did I really have a choice? The mirror possessed me and that is where it all began. I wanted to search through that trunk. Maybe I could find some answers.

I questioned Joe, "Did you see that mirror Nathaniel took out of the trunk?"

"No, I didn't. I heard you scream my name and came running over. Why?"

Joanna spoke up then, "Mom, I saw it. I was watching you from across the room. That mirror looked just like the one hanging in your hallway — the one that is warm to the touch and makes a humming sound. Is that what caused you to faint?"

"I think so. It was a shock to me, like the mirror was following us!" I didn't mean to say that part out loud and with the snickering from Tom and Joanna, I knew I should not have.

"Come on, Mom, you make it sound like the mirror is stalking you!" Joanna poked fun at me but they did not know the full story.

For a moment I wanted to tell them about Annabelle and later on in the bedroom I discussed it with Joe. The kids had enough to worry about during their six-month stay, so we decided to remain quiet until there were some firm answers. I needed to talk with Henry and Phillip. Thank goodness in this day and age with cell phones and subscribing to unlimited global long distance, I could call them and talk as long as I wanted with no monetary burden. Tomorrow I would call them, after figuring out the time difference as I didn't want to call in the middle of the night. In the meantime, I would get up early in the morning and complete my family tree, as much as I could.

Chapter Twenty-Two

The morning was bright and crisp. For the winter season, this day felt more like a beautiful autumn morning back home. I was awake before anyone else. Thank goodness I had a restful sleep with no dreams whatsoever. Once the coffee was done, I poured a large cup and added England's version of half and half, my usual drink, but I preferred the half and half back home. England's was too heavy for me. Joanna had brought her computer out to the dining room table before she went to sleep last night so I had a roomy space to work. London was six hours later than Minneapolis. It was now 7:00 in the morning, so I had time to work on my family tree before I called Henry and Phillip. In a few hours they would be done working and hopefully had time to chat. First, I signed onto my yahoo.com account to check my email. There were several emails from Lexi and Donna begging me to update them on our trip. I would need to call them too.

I had no ill effects from my brief fainting spell the night before, so I grabbed a writing tablet and pen and signed onto Ancestry.com. I pulled up the family tree I previously started. We did not have access in the house to a printer so I wrote down the information on paper. My maiden name was Clark. Dad's side of the family already had a family tree created, and there was nothing questionable there. Recapping my mother's side, she, Elizabeth

Smith, married Robert Clark in 1941 at the age of twenty. They tried, unsuccessfully, for ten years to have a child. Finally, at age thirty, she gave birth to me.

My maternal grandfather, Edward Smith, married Mary Fisher in 1893. She was only seventeen. My grandfather, Edward, had been in the United States less than a year when they wed. After he left Sweden, I remember hearing stories that when he met Mary, he fell head over heels in love with her. He never looked at another woman, so they said. They had a happy marriage and raised five children. My, mother, Elizabeth, was their last-born child. The story was that my grandfather, Edward, never returned to Sweden and never saw his parents, Margaret and Albert, again. So sad. I wondered what happened there. It must have been some story, but I never heard what it was. I tried to search for a birth certificate for my Great-grandmother Margaret using her married name of Smith but could not find any. I'm not sure back then if they even had records of births. Realizing I never knew my great-grandmother's maiden name, the feeling of futility came over me. Was this never discussed with my parents during my youth? Then again, I never met my great-grandmother as she lived in Sweden. I only knew the afghan in my living room was made by her and handed down to me. This had to be an area that needed to be researched. What happened back then with Edward leaving Sweden in 1892, never seeing his family again? Why did the family tree end there, with my great-grandmother? I decided to rest my eyes from the computer. Everyone else except Joanna were slowly rising and wanting breakfast. I took a break and joined them in the kitchen for a few minutes before making my phone calls.

*   *   *

Joanna was sleeping in. Tom said she wasn't feeling good. She was up most of the night and had thrown up a few times this morning. I went in the bedroom to check on her. She was asleep. I felt her forehead and cheeks. She did not seem to have a fever. It could just be the changes in climate and food.

I told Tom and Joe they could go about exploring London if they wanted to. I would stay in with Joanna as I had phone calls to make and research to do. After Tom and Joe left, I called Lexi and Donna. Lexi was thrilled to hear from me, wanting to know what we had seen as tourists, and how our trip was going. She was excited for me to come back and get her all caught up. (Note to myself: Pick up souvenir gifts for friends). Next, I called Donna. Before I could tell her anything about our trip, she interrupted to let me know she had driven by our home daily to be sure it was still standing due to the mirror.

"Rest assured, Anna, if anything happens to your house, I will handle it."

Oh course, she would. That was Donna.

108

"There is no need to do that, Donna. I'm sure everything will be OK."

"Well," Donna sounded a little put off. "With that mirror and paranormal activity happening in your home, who knows?"

"You haven't told anybody about it, have you Donna?" I squirmed, just knowing she would be in her glory to be the first one to tell people. Sometimes you confide in people — afterwards, you feel it may have been a mistake.

"No, I haven't, but you need to take care of that soon. I can't believe you left with that thing in your house!"

"We will be home soon, no worries." I couldn't wait to get her off the phone.

Next, I called Henry. My dear, old friend Henry was so happy to hear from me. He was concerned how everything was going and if we had the chance to do much research. I summarized for him where we were so far. When I told him about the old trunk and the mirror that looked so much like the one hanging on my wall, it sounded like his breath stopped as he hesitated and warned me to be careful.

"There has to be a connection, Anna. What other explanation can there be? Remember, you may not be happy with what you find. Years ago, people were not so open about family secrets."

I told him not to worry as I had family all around to support me. He seemed to calm down when I told him I would be calling Phillip next.

While on the phone with Phillip, he told me he was continuing with research whenever he had time, but as of yet, he had not come up with much information. His contacts in Europe were now 99% sure the mirror came from England, not France, circa early to mid 1800's. Phillip suggested I visit some additional historical places where I might find similar styles of the mirror and would be able to inquire as to their origin.

After my phone calls, I was mentally fatigued. So many suggestions and so many opinions, it was confusing and yet I did feel closer to finding the truth. It had to be with my great-grandmother, but she was from Sweden and all indications were that the mirror was from England.

Joanna was now awake, and I decided to spend time with her while the guys were out. She said she felt better but still, she looked tired. I offered to make her breakfast, but she said the thought of eggs turned her stomach. She settled for toast with some raspberry jam. She didn't want coffee, only water to drink.

"You must have caught a bug, or do you think it's just a reaction to the change in time and food?" I wasn't too concerned, but I wanted her to get better before we left in a week.

"Mom, between you and me, and ONLY between you and me, if I didn't know better, I would swear I was pregnant!"

My mouth literally dropped open! "Honey, are you sure?"

"No, Mom, and please promise me you won't mention anything to Dad or Tom, until I'm sure."

"OK, but when was your last period?"

"Well, a few weeks before we left, I had one, but it was so light and lasted only a day and a half."

I had known since Joanna started her periods at the age of fourteen that they had always been heavy and lasted a solid week.

"Joanna, aren't you using birth control pills?" The pills had calmed her cramps and length of her period but not to only a day and a half.

"Yes, I admit I did miss taking them a few times in the last month with all the hectic activity for this trip, but that's happened before, and I didn't get pregnant. I don't know. It seems like I've had nausea episodes since we last stayed at your house." She smirked.

"Honey, if you're not feeling better by the time we leave, I think you should fly home with us to see your doctor. Being in a foreign place, I don't like the idea of you seeing a brand-new doctor who is unaware of your history. Daddy and I can buy your ticket, and I'm sure Tom would agree. You can always fly back after you find out what's wrong and then find a doctor in London for the interim.

"Well," Joanna said. "Let's not jump to conclusions. Like you said, it could be the difference in food, climate, and time."

Just then we heard the car pull in, and Joanna pleaded with me again to keep this only between us. I agreed, for now.

Chapter Twenty-Three

The following afternoon, Nathaniel and Catherine came over for lunch. I had worked on my family tree the night before. I wanted to simplify as much information as I could. After I drew an elementary looking family tree free hand, it did seem simpler than I had antagonized over. I said a little prayer hoping the St. Martins would be able to help fill in the missing pieces.

After a light lunch consisting of a variety of salads purchased at a local deli, some mixed fruit, and bagels baked fresh that morning at a nearby bakery, we started going over our notes. Nathaniel and Catherine told us they had spent much time going through his mother's old trunk. To Nathaniel's surprise he came across a number of journals filled with notes about tracing the family roots and trying to locate a missing child. It seemed a shame Nathaniel's mother had worked so hard at this in her later years and passed away, not discovering anything concrete. Or did she, and we were the ones who had yet to discover it?

I laid out my family tree, explaining the missing piece I had was of my Great-grandmother Margaret, born in 1837. It was a dead end.

"Wait a minute," Catherine exclaimed. "In Nathaniel's mother's journal, she mentioned several attempts to track down a missing child born in England sometime in 1837."

"That is sad, but it couldn't be related to my great-grandmother as she was born in Sweden."

"To my knowledge," Nathaniel said, "they never did find that child."

Timidly I asked, "Do you mind if I look through your mother's journals?"

"Of course not! That's why we brought them. We haven't even finished reading all of them so maybe we can still find out something."

"Nathaniel, do you have the family tree that your mother started? Could I study it?"

He gave me the hand-written papers. As he mentioned earlier, it was difficult to read his late mother's handwriting. I was unfamiliar with some of her acronyms and abbreviations. Most of it I could figure out but the fading ink from the past several years did not help. After studying the partially diminished script, I could tell Nathaniel's mother's family tree, like my father's, was fairly straight forward. The St. Martin's side was the one that had been seeking a missing child. The notes explained how Nathaniel's mother, Rose, had continued the task, after all these years, to track down the child. It had been a request of her late husband's once he was too ill to continue. It was amazing to see how Nathaniel's father, grandfather, and great-grandfather had all attempted to track down what happened to this baby born in England in 1837.

It was approaching evening, and the St. Martin's needed to leave. They left the journals with me to study, and we agreed to meet again in a few days.

That night, I stayed up all night trying to decipher the journals. Then, I came across a letter tucked into one of the first journals. It had been wrapped in what appeared to be wax paper. I pulled it out and carefully opened it, twitching at the crackling of the ancient, yellowed paper. It was addressed on military stationery to Mister Samuel and Genevieve St. Martin. The signatures were unclear, but the summary of what I could read in this sorrowful and heartbreaking letter was very clear.

Calvary Record Office
<u>This fourteenth day of October, eighteen
hundred and thirty-seven</u>

Mister Samuel and Genevieve St. Martin,

It is my painful duty to inform you
that a report has been received from the War
office notifying the death of:
(No.) <u>19510102</u>
(Rank) <u>Corporal</u>
(Name) <u>Richard St. Martin</u>
(Regiment) <u>20th Brigade</u>
(which occurred) <u>at the military base
hospital in Spain</u>
(On the) <u>twenty-eighth day of September,
eighteen hundred and thirty-seven</u>
The report is to the effect that he <u>died due
to complications of war injuries suffered
during the Spanish Conflict of the Carlist
War.</u>
By Her Majesty's command I am to
forward the enclosed message of sympathy
from Her Gracious Majesty Queen Victoria.
I am to add that any information that may
be received as to the soldier's burial will
be communicated in due course. A separate
leaflet dealing more fully with this subject
is enclosed.
I am,
<u>Special</u> xxxxxxxxx
Your Obedient Servant,
 corp pet
Office in Charge of Records

How sad back then it took so long to inform loved ones on the death of a family member. There was no leaflet attached but I wondered what the military did with bodies of soldiers that died in a war fought not on their home turf. I googled it and shuddered at the thought of mass graves and having your child buried God knows where. How sad for these parents.

Then, it hit me! This soldier's name was Richard! Could this be Annabelle's Richard? She was pregnant and gave birth in 1837. Did she know of Richard's death? I had to speak more with Nathaniel. It was early in the morning. 3:00 am. I hadn't yet slept. I thought of waking Joe. Instead, I laid in bed, too excited to sleep and contemplated if I had found the "link".

I wondered if Annabelle had felt abandoned, remembering how she asked me, "What happened to Richard?" Then I realized that she must have known as the words in the poem hidden in the mirror came back to me, "duty causes much pain" and "in heaven we will meet again someday."

Richard must have known he was dying. Did he know Annabelle was pregnant? I felt I was unraveling Annabelle's case, but how could I possibly be related to Nathaniel? That was still a mystery.

It was now 5:30 in the morning. I got up and made coffee, excited to share these details with Joe.

Chapter Twenty-Four

Joanna was feeling better. She got up about 7:00 am and joined me for breakfast.

"You look happy today," she smiled at me.

"Well, I stayed up all night looking through Nathaniel's mother's journals. I still can't figure out how we could be related, but it was fascinating looking at letters from the mid 1800's. Lots of history in those journals, and I do wish I paid more attention in school during history class. I read a letter about a war during Queen Victoria's reign. It was called The Carlist War, and I don't remember even studying that one."

"I don't either, Mom. Did you google it?"

"I did but I thought by then I should get some sleep. But that didn't happen."

We both laughed.

Joanna had poured herself a cup of coffee and was eating a cinnamon roll from the bakery. All of a sudden, she looked ill. She ran to the bathroom and I followed. I held back her hair as she vomited into the toilet. Once she was done, Joanna said she felt better.

"Honey," I whispered excitedly in her ear, "I think you are pregnant!"

"I am beginning to think so more and more. I've been having dreams again about a baby, but this time the baby is a healthy, happy little girl!" She giggled.

"OK, I will keep quiet for now, as promised, but I want you to fly home with us. Let's tell Tom and Joe you just want to see your doctor back home and once checked out, you will return to London."

After Joe and Tom had their coffee, Joanna started the conversation of flying home with us to see her doctor.

Tom looked a little confused asking, "Gee, Honey, can't you simply phone your doctor and see if they have any recommendations over here?"

"Yes, Tom, I could do that, but honestly why would they? This is another country. I can't believe I didn't think of getting copies of both of our clinic records knowing we would be here for six months, in case anything happened."

"Joanna," Tom said with concern. "Is there something you aren't telling me?"

"Heavens, no. I just feel stupid I didn't think of it before we left and as I haven't been feeling so good, I would rather check things out back home with my own doctor."

"Well, I should come with you."

"Tom, Mom and Dad will be with me. You need to stay here and spend time with Jon before art classes begin. I'll be fine. I'm a big girl."

Joanna winked at Tom and smiled, but I sensed Tom was not too happy about it.

After breakfast, as Joanna was feeling better, she went with Tom to do some sight-seeing while Joe and I stayed home. I was sure Tom wanted to question her more in private.

Once they were gone, Joe asked, "What was that all about?"

"Well, I didn't get a chance to talk with you before they were awake, but I think it's a good idea, don't you? After all, Joanna should have thought about bringing copies of their medical records, and she will have us along in case she still isn't feeling good."

"Anna, we live in Minnesota, and Joanna lives out East!"

I knew then I had to break my promise. What else could I do? "OK, Joe, first you are sworn to secrecy. If you let Joanna know I told you this, I will never forgive you, and you can't tell Tom either."

Joe nodded his head, eagerly waiting for what I was about to tell him.

"Joanna thinks she might be pregnant! She doesn't want you or Tom to know until she is absolutely certain. She will need copies of her records in case she is so I suggested she fly home with us. I would like to spend some time with her as she will be gone for six months. I would be willing to stay with her so she has someone with her when she goes to the doctor."

Joe nodded while a grin materialized on his face that then turned into a smile from ear to ear. "Anna, that would be great, but I don't like the idea of keeping something this important from Tom. He should know, and he should be the one to go with Joanna."

"You're probably right, Joe. I think Joanna may be afraid to take him away from his work. Let me talk with her and try to convince her to tell him. Meanwhile, mums the word, Grandpa."

*   *   *

Joe wanted to take a walk after that. Realizing I hadn't yet told him about the journals, I briefly conveyed what I had learned. I wanted to call the St. Martin's so I told Joe to go ahead on his walk.

I reached Nathaniel and explained as best as I could over the phone what I uncovered. He was excited to enlighten me on some history he had recently unearthed.

"Anna, I am ashamed to admit that I too was not a good student of my own country's history. I think now I will read up on it to educate myself better. I read more letters from my mother's trunk and then went on the internet to fill in what I did not know. In 1837, King William IV died. In June of that year, his niece was crowned Queen Victoria of Britain. She was only seventeen years old. That began the Victorian age. Queen Victoria refused guidance from her domineering mother. She ruled in her own stead. Respect for the crown was at a low point during her coronation, but in her modest and straightforward way, the young Queen won over the hearts of her subjects. Not having any direct input in policy decisions, nevertheless, she respectfully demanded to be informed of all political matters. During her reign, from 1837 – 1901, the British army was called upon to participate in many wars, including military expeditions and action in different parts of the world. Many British soldiers were killed in these wars and unfortunately, they are now hardly mentioned or remembered."

"Nathaniel, do you think that is what happened to Richard? Did you know who Richard was?"

"I only know what I am learning as I read these letters. Apparently, Richard was my great-grandfather's child. He fought in the first of three Carlist Wars."

I interrupted Nathaniel. "What is a Carlist War? I've never heard of it."

"The Carlist War was a civil war in Spain. This one was from 1833 to 1840. It was a war of succession, questioning who the rightful successor to King Ferdinand VII of Spain was. The Carlists' goal was to return to an absolute monarchy. The Liberals sought to defend the constitutional monarchy. Portugal, France, and United Kingdom sent volunteers and regular forces to confront the Carlist army. Richard St. Martin died in that war, and from what I can decipher from my mother's information, he was in love and planned on getting married as soon as he was released from the army. Apparently, his fiancé was pregnant and that was not a good thing in nineteenth century England. He wrote his mother begging her to contact his fiancé to protect her and the child."

"Nathaniel, do you know what happened to her and the baby?" My heart was racing as this mystery was become unraveled.

"I haven't found anything yet with her name, however, her baby was the one everyone searched for with unsuccessful results. Let's get together soon and maybe compare our notes? You have only a week left, right?"

"Yes, we leave in a week and a half, and I would like to gather as much information as possible. I'm still not sure how we are related."

"Anna, I had Ancestry.com do my DNA test again. It came back the same, so somehow, some time ago, we must have been family. We need to keep in touch with each other regardless of what we do or don't discover."

"Thank you, Nathaniel. It means a lot to me."

"Would you please start calling me 'Nat'. That 'Nathaniel' name is too formal."

"It's a deal. Are you and Catherine available for dinner tomorrow night? I will check with Joe to be sure. I want to give Joanna and Tom an evening to themselves before we leave.

Sometimes as an adult you can get too much of your parents." We both laughed.

"Yes. Let's plan on it. I'll call you in the morning to be sure. Meantime, I've got more exploring to do in that trunk."

Once I was off the phone, I went to the computer to find out what it was like to be pregnant and unmarried in England during the 1800's. The details were horrible! A woman in this condition was a disgrace to her family. She was shamed and sent to a "Home". Her baby would be taken away. One such place was The Foundling Hospital. It is now a museum in London. The articles I read did not indicate what happened to or where the unwed mother would live. If her family was disgraced, she most likely took refuge in such a home until the child was born. The stigma put upon these women was horrible, and not surprising, the article mentioned that such stigma did not apply to unmarried fathers. I decided Joe and I needed to visit this museum. My heart was beating so fast, I knew I was on the brink of something.

Chapter Twenty-Five

Pleased that Joe came back from his walk before Joanna and Tom returned, I took advantage of that time to talk with him. After I informed him about Richard St. Martin and his then pregnant fiancé, my hope was he would agree to follow this through with me.

"Joe, would you be willing to have dinner with the St. Martin's tomorrow night? Things are starting to come together and I feel we have to tell them about the mirror and Annabelle. Annabelle must have been Richard's fiancé."

Joe let out a long, whistled sigh. He was in deep, serious thought. Finally, he reluctantly agreed with the conditions that we not involve Tom and Joanna. At that point, he didn't want Joanna concerned about anything except her health. We had not yet told her about Annabelle.

"What I should do, Joe, is speak with Joanna later today and try to persuade her to have dinner with Tom tomorrow night — just the two of them. I will try to convince her it would be a perfect time for her to tell Tom exactly why she will be coming home with us."

Joe agreed.

"Remember, if Joanna decides to tell Tom and possibly you, you are to act surprised."

"Yes, Dear. Seems like I'm always agreeing to or falling into your schemes."

We smiled at each other knowing, as we discussed privately many times, we were experiencing something unbelievable and unimaginable. How could the scenario of the past two months of our lives ever be explained?

Just in time, we wrapped up our talk as Joanna and Tom came home. Joanna no longer looked ill. They had a great time exploring shops. She bought the cutest salt and pepper shakers that looked like the red phone booths in London. Years ago, those red phone booths were really something. Now, with everyone having cell phones, they are used like small kiosks and newspaper stands on the streets of London. Joanna's purchases gave me an idea!

"Joanna, I know you are most likely too tired today, but maybe in the morning you and I could go shopping. It wouldn't be for long as I just want to buy a few souvenirs for my friends."

"Sure, maybe we could even go after dinner tonight as the shops are open later."

= =

After dinner, Joanne said she still felt like going out. Tom told us to go shopping, and he would do the dishes and clean up the kitchen. Joe didn't offer but I knew he would help Tom. So, Joanna and I were off on our shopping trip. Now, how would I bring up what I needed to talk to her about?

Joanna took me back to the shop where she found the little salt and pepper shakers. I bought several sets. I wanted one as well as giving sets to my friends. Next, we went to a shop specializing in gifts with a "Royalty Theme". There were items with past and current royal families' pictures. I purchased a round pill box for my purse. It had a picture on top of Queen Victoria. I thought that it was quite appropriate. I talked Joanna into sitting down inside a little café for dessert. So many choices! I decided on a Bakewell Tart. It was a delicious short crust pastry with a layer of raspberry jam and sponge cake with ground almonds. Joanna indulged in a slice of Banoffee Pie, which our waiter told us was a typical English dessert pie made from bananas, cream, and toffee from boiled condensed milk. We had a bite of each other's, and the Banoffee Pie was soft and yummy. My dessert was lighter but I'm sure the calorie count was not. A cup of British tea went perfectly with our sinfully delicious desserts! Halfway through after many mmm's and yum's, I approached the topic I needed to. Joanna listened without interruption. She thought about it and said, "Mom, I was actually feeling guilty keeping this from Tom. If I am pregnant, he should be the first to know, after me of course. I don't want him to take time off his study. That is the reason we came here. That, and spending Christmas in 'Merry Old England'."

"I have been so wrapped up in getting to know the St. Martins and how we could be related, I haven't thought much of Christmas!

Now, going to the stores and seeing all the decorations, I need to get busy as we only have a few days left."

"Relax, Mom, that is one of the reasons you and Dad came here. Remember? No hassle with Christmas lights, no holiday stress."

"You're right honey. Well, I know what I want to get your dad for Christmas. One of those nice Burberry men's scarves to keep him warm. What do you think Tom would like?"

"I got him a pair of nice leather gloves. You know, I bet Tom would like one of those scarves too. I know they're kind of spendy."

"Don't worry about that! I have to treat my son-in-law right, especially if he is going to be a daddy. So, Joanna, what do you think? Are you going to tell Tom?"

"Have you told Dad?"

I crossed my fingers under the table as I replied, "No, honey, I'm waiting for you to tell him. We are going to have dinner with the St. Martin's tomorrow night. Why don't you and Tom have a nice quiet dinner, just the two of you, and talk to him."

"OK, I guess I will. I know he needs to spend more time with Jon, and after the holidays he will, so it may be a perfect time for me to go home. You plan on leaving January 2nd, right? After New Year's?"

"Yes, so we need to know as soon as possible to be sure we can get your ticket. Gosh, Christmas is in a few days. I wonder if Joe has thought about it?"

"Mom, I know they went Christmas shopping the other day."

"Why those little sneaks! We have to figure out dinner plans! OK, let's go get those scarves and have them gift wrapped. Also, let's pick up some cookies, a little tree, and some decorations."

"Oh, Mom, don't get stressed out!"

"Hey, it wouldn't be Christmas without stress."

We walked back to the bungalow, arm in arm with our packages, singing along with the carolers who were performing on the streets. There still wasn't snow, but the weather was getting chilly and damp. Instead of snow, we felt cloaked in typical London fog.

Once home, Joanna and I set up our little tabletop tree, still singing a few Christmas carols slightly off-key. I must admit back in the States the selection of ornaments is much better. We have more bling, even if all that bling is imported from other countries. The guys were teasing us, saying neither one of us could ever 'not' celebrate Christmas, or make a living as a singer. We discussed the holiday meals, as we had not made any reservations anywhere and thought it would be too late. Tom said Jon invited all of us to join him and his parents on New Year's Eve. They had reservations and a full day and night planned. It was their gift to us to see London at its finest. Earlier we had all decided to leave three days between Christmas and New Year's to visit different tourist spots. I wanted to go to The Foundling Hospital, and one day Jon was taking us into

France via the Chunnel. We left New Year's open, so we agreed it would be fun.

"Tom, what on earth do they have planned that's going to take all day?" I could not imagine.

"I know Jon got tickets to 'The Playhouse Theatre', a nice dinner, and I found it strange they had to get tickets to see the 'fireworks'. I guess London has some of the best fireworks in the world on New Year's Eve. It should be a fun experience. I have no idea what we are seeing at the theatre."

"How nice of them. We need to pay them something. How can they afford this?" I didn't want to take advantage of their hospitality.

Tom smiled and said, "I know. I felt the same but trust me, Jon won't accept anything. He has connections through the University and the Art scene. He wants to do this and any attempt to repay him may be an insult."

Joanna looked at me and asked, "Mom, do you have anything to wear that would be fancy enough to go to the theatre and dinner?"

Tom said, "Jon told me dress would be 'business casual'. Dad, no need to wear a tie. I think you can wear the sports coat you brought. That's what I plan on wearing." He then looked at Joanna, "Honey, you're fine with some of the clothes you brought, but we're going to be here for six months. So if you want to get something new, you should."

Joanna turned to me, "Want to go shopping again."

"I did bring one dress I could wear, but I'm always up for shopping."

Chapter Twenty-Six

Joe and I decided to go Christmas shopping together the next afternoon before meeting up with the St. Martins for dinner. I told him what I bought for Tom. He thought it was a nice gift. Walking down the streets of the shopping district, we passed the Burberry store. He saw the scarf displayed in the window.

"Is that what you got Tom?" Joe asked.

"Yes. Do you like it?"

"I should buy one for myself."

Hmm…. I wondered if he suspected what I'd gotten for him. "I think you should wait until December 26th. It may go on sale."

"OK, but what are we going to get for Joanna? She's our only child, and they are letting us stay in the bungalow for free. I would like to get both of them something special. Don't get me wrong, the scarf is striking, but maybe we should also get them a gift certificate while they're here."

As I was thinking, I glanced in the window of the Burberry store and a beautiful briefcase caught my eye.

"Let's go in here."

I picked up the briefcase, telling Joe it would be perfect for Tom. The sign identified it as a "Men's Marley TB-Monogram Laptop Case". Well, it was more than that. It had padded space for a laptop and a roomy area for papers, books, etc. The briefcase had a numeric lock that you could change as desired. It was sizeable but not ostentatious or showy. It was dark brown with kind of a subtle crisscross pattern. Nice and soft, it felt like lambskin.

Joe checked out the price tag and whistled, "Wow, Anna, you can't be serious! Look at the price!"

"Oh my," I felt somewhat deflated. The price was $1,049.00.

Just then a well-dressed saleswoman approached us. "May I help you?"

Joe left it to me to chat with her. "We were looking for a nice gift for our son-in-law".

"My name is Linda, and I would be happy to help you. This is a lovely case. You can have it monogrammed at no extra cost."

Joe couldn't help himself, "Well, for over a thousand dollars, it should be free!"

Linda smiled, "I understand. This is a high-end product, but Burberry has a lifetime guarantee if anything happens to the leather, straps, or lock simply bring it back to our store, and we ship it to the factory for repair. If it cannot be repaired, we replace it with a new bag."

"You wouldn't be able to get it monogrammed in time for Christmas, would you?" I asked.

I looked at Joe who was staring at me like I had lost my mind.

"No," Linda replied, "But your son-in-law could bring it back after the holidays, and it could be monogrammed in only a few days."

Looking at Joe, I didn't want to start World War III right in the Burberry store, "We'll think about it. I want to look around some more."

Linda was nice, not too pushy. "Sure, let me know if you have any questions."

I wanted to continue looking around the store. Joe thought the pricing in this store was ridiculous and said he would wait outside.

In the corner of the store were several purses on sale. I spotted something that would be perfect for Joanna, and the pattern matched the scarf I had already gotten for Tom. It was a Hackberry Check Canvas Crossbody Bag. The original price was $970. That was a lot of money for an item smaller than the brief case and made out of canvas instead of leather. The sale sign said 30% off. That would bring it down to about $680. Still expensive.

Linda came over and asked if I was interested in the sale bag. I told her it was still too much money, even with the 30% discount.

"You can also get this one monogrammed." She then picked up a wallet that matched the purse. "This wallet was originally $230 and is also 30% off. It would go perfectly with the purse and fits nicely inside, leaving enough space for other items."

"I don't know. I'll have to speak with my husband about it."

Linda nodded knowingly, "We are a high-end store. Our merchandise is beautiful and popular, so of course prices reflect that. What I can do for you is if you decide to purchase the briefcase and the purse, I will give you the wallet at no charge."

"That would be great! So, are you indicating there is some 'wiggle room' in your pricing?"

"Only on the inventory that is on sale."

"Let me talk with Joe, and I'll let you know."

I led Joe to the small café where Joanna and I had devoured those luscious desserts. I told Joe about the purse and wallet, but he still thought we would be spending too much money on Christmas gifts.

"Joe, have you spent much money on a gift for me?"

"Not yet. I picked up a little something for you, but I was going to go out on my own before Christmas. What about you, did you spend much money on me?"

"I bought you one nice gift. Regardless, think about this, Joe. How much money would we have spent for a place to stay these two weeks?"

"What's your point, Anna?"

"I was thinking we are not going to see the kids for six months after this. I thought if we didn't buy each other anything else and purchased that bag for Tom and the purse for Joanna, it would be something they could be so proud of and a nice memory for them. The gifts would be good for years to come. Isn't that what Christmas should be about? Let's do it. If you need rationalizing, think of it as the hotel money we didn't need. Don't you want to create memories and not think of money?"

"Yes, but creating your type of memories always seems to cost money!"

He chuckled so I knew he had given in. We walked back to the store. Linda was pleased to see us. She told us if we came back in an hour, our purchases would be beautifully gift wrapped. Joe took out his wallet and pulled out our American Express Card. As Linda was ringing up the sale, Joe surprised me by saying, "So, we are spending over a thousand dollars plus the scarf you already bought for Tom, but only about $700 on Anna. We need to get something else for Anna."

I was shocked! I think Linda was too. The Christmas Spirit had entered Tom's soul!

After a few silent moments, Linda said, "Oh, I have an idea!"

No one else was in the store at that time. Linda told us after Christmas she was putting all the women's cashmere scarves on sale. She would be willing to sell us one now for 50% off, but we could not let other people know. She would need to ring it up as a separate purchase and run it through the day of the sale, however, she was willing to let us take it today.

"I bought a scarf here a few days ago for my son-in-law. I Guess I should have waited."

Linda quickly added, "It's only certain colors, not our classic design. Let me show you."

She brought out colors of blue plaid and beige. I liked the blue plaid but it wouldn't go with the purse we picked out for Joanna.

"You know what?" Joe cut in. "Let's get her a scarf to match the purse. We're spending enough money that a few hundred dollars more won't matter."

I let Joe pick out the scarf, and to my surprise, it was the same pattern as the ones I purchased earlier. Joe said he really liked it, and now Joanna and Tom would match as well as the purse.

Joe and I went back to the café to have dessert and coffee. Joe was not a tea drinker.

"You know, Anna, I am numb about spending all this money, but I know this is a special year, and like you said, 'Let's create memories!' Are you happy?"

Looking into Joe's eyes and smiling, I replied, "Very happy, Joe. Are you?"

He grasped my hand and said, "I always have been since the day we met."

Changing the subject, he asked, "How does it feel not to be thinking about Annabelle?"

"Funny that I haven't thought about her most of the day, but we need to tell the St. Martins about it tonight."

Joe grinned and nodded, "Why not? Let someone else think we've lost our minds."

We finished our desserts and walked back to the store. Our packages were ready and so beautifully wrapped in gold foil with silver and gold ribbons and glittery deep red bows. Walking back to the bungalow, hand in hand, I realized how fortunate I was to have such a loving husband, daughter, and son-in-law. I felt as if a weight had been lifted off my shoulders by no longer fearing whatever the outcome would be from Annabelle and my heredity. I still wanted to pursue the mystery, but I knew I was blessed, whatever the outcome. Suddenly, I remembered what Annabelle said to me, "We are only a breath away." I knew I would be thankful to find out the truth but realized life is short and in only a breath a baby lives and in only that last breath we die.

Chapter Twenty-Seven

I was thankful the St. Martins suggested a casual restaurant but then most of the London eateries seemed generally casual. Christmas was the following day. I was getting an itch to go into France on the Chunnel later in the week. Relaying my fear to Nat (as he now wanted me to call him), he asked what I was afraid of.

"Nat, we will be going under water into the ocean, from one country to another! What's not to be afraid of?"

Everyone else chuckled. Nat tried to convince me I would never even know I was underwater. I would have to wait and see.

All of us thought it would be best if we enjoyed our dinner and then hashed over what each of us had discovered. There was a pub near the restaurant that Catherine said was unusually quiet providing we got in there before 7:00 pm. We munched on our burgers and fries, or I should say burgers and "chips". Not as good as in the USA, but I didn't complain.

Heading over to the pub, I noticed Nat carrying a duffel bag that seemed to be loaded with papers. I only had a tote bag with my notes and journals from Nat's mother to return to him. After settling into a booth nestled back in a corner, Nat insisted on buying the first round. First round? I thought. I didn't usually drink beer. I am more of a wine drinker. Nat insisted I at least try the most popular beer in London. Catherine seemed to be knowledgeable on London's Pub history. She told us Pubs were a classic part of London's social life and that the best beer was called Porter. Porter is a dark style of beer made from brown malt. The name was first recorded in the 18th century. The name Porter was believed to come from its popularity with street and river porters, who carried objects for others.

Catherine thought I would like it. She described its flavor as having an aroma of chocolate and malt loaf — whatever that was — and tasted smooth and fruity with a light bite of roasted malt with hints of vanilla.

"Wow! Am I impressed!" I told her.

"Oh no, don't be. Our son, Jon, is a beer connoisseur, and he's taught us so much about it."

I didn't think I would like the beer, but I liked chocolate! The first sip I took, I must have made a sour or unpleasant face as everyone in the booth laughed at me.

"It's so strong!" I shouted. Laughter erupted all around as well as from the bar.

"Hey, I'm a good sport. I'll take more than one sip."

The more I sipped, the better it tasted, but if there was any chocolate in this beer, it was a weird tasting chocolate. There is no way I would be able to drink even one mug of this. Joe was a sweetheart and went up to the bar to get me a class of white wine. I didn't know Pubs had wine, but it is only a very limited house selection. Anything was better than the Porter. Joe said he would drink the rest of my beer.

After a few moments of chatter, it was time to get down to business. I wanted to get my cards out on the table first. I explained to the St. Martins my unusual find and attraction to the mirror along with our paranormal experiences, and the look on both of their faces exhibited much doubt and reservation. They remained quiet for several minutes while each one of us sipped our beverages, fearful of making eye contact with each other.

Thank goodness for Joe! He broke the silence, "Look, I know how hard this is to comprehend and believe. I was the biggest skeptic of all! Then, I witnessed what Anna had been trying to convince me of. Please, just hear us out! Let's look at both family trees and see if anything falls in place. Are you both willing to do that before you decide we need to go to the 'funny farm'?"

Nat cleared his throat, and Catherine placed her hand gently on his. She smiled, kind of a sad smile, and Nat nodded at her indicating permission for her to continue.

"We don't think you need to go to any 'funny farm'. It is hard to believe, however, we found additional journals and letters in Nat's mother's trunk that may give credence to what you are saying. I've often wondered what happens after we die. I personally have not ever seen any spirits but, I'm hoping they are out there. Nat has told me many times that he hears his grandfather speak to him. I would hate it if after we die that is all there is." Catherine crossed her arms, rubbing the upper part of them as if she were chilled.

Nat pulled out the journals, letters, and notes for display on the table.

"Anna, may I see your family tree, please?"

I pulled out my handwritten papers. I showed him where I struck a dead end with my Great-grandmother, Margaret. Then, I let him read the letter that was in one of the journals — the notice of Richard St. Martin's death.

Nat placed his family tree next to mine. He was in deep thought comparing them. "I probably shouldn't have any more beer while trying to decipher this." He laughed. "I do believe, Anna, that you and I are distantly related. You see, your dead end, as you say, is with your Great-grandmother, Margaret, who was born in 1837. Your mystery is on your maternal side. Where my information seems to become a mystery is on my fraternal side with my Great-grandparent's son, Richard St. Martin. I remember my grandfather telling me how his father and mother, Samuel and Genevieve, had lost a son in the army. I never heard much about it. It was so long ago."

We were all silent for a while trying to absorb all these generations. It was somewhat confusing.

I suggested we concentrate on the year 1837.

"My Great-grandmother, Margaret, was born that year, and that was the same year Richard was killed. You said you had letters from Richard begging his mother to watch over his pregnant fiancé."

"Yes," Nat said but I didn't think he was grasping where I was going with this.

"You told me that it was a horrible time to be pregnant and not married. I looked up on the internet to see what happened to unwed mothers in England back then. Many were sent to The Foundling Hospital, and it is now a museum. I think we need to go there and check it out. Maybe they have records way back then of babies born there. What do you think?"

"It sounds reasonable, but Anna, don't you think my grandparents and those before would have checked that out?"

"Not necessarily," Catherine cut in. "Back then it was shameful, and families banished their children. Too bad we didn't know Richard's fiancé's surname or even her given first name."

"I'm not sure it would matter," Nat spoke up. "I remember studying in school that the British Government performed the first census in 1801. The Industrial Revolution was underway and the population was over sixteen million. Surprisingly, with all those people, only 300 surnames were known."

"Is that why the English people have so many common names like Smith and Jones?" I asked.

"Wait a minute!" Finally, Joe put a word in. "Your maiden name is Smith. You wondered why your great-grandmother was born in Sweden, but she married a Smith. Did they meet in Sweden, with a name like Smith? I'll bet there aren't many Smith's that come from Sweden!"

My head was swimming. Maybe it was the wine. Joe must have sensed it as he said, "Let's call it a night. Maybe we can do some research between Christmas and New Year's."

"That's a good idea," I agreed. "I know we are going into France on the Chunnel in a few days, but do you think we could visit The Foundling Museum before we have to fly home?" I wasn't asking anyone in particular but everyone assumed my question was directed toward Nat.

"Why not?" Nat was a trooper. He would call the museum to see what their holiday hours were and get back to us. We wished them a Merry Christmas and told them how much we looked forward to New Year's Eve with them. I asked Catherine what the dress attire would be. She told me not to worry about buying anything new. Nowadays people didn't care how dressy you were unless it was to see the Queen. I returned Nat's journals to him and he handed me a shoebox he had been carrying in his duffle bag. He told me it was filled with letters and notes he had not yet read. I told him I would be happy to search through them. We all said our goodbyes and headed back.

Chapter Twenty-Eight

I decided not to read any more letters until after Christmas. I wanted to spend time with our family. Joanna had told Tom about the possibility of her pregnancy. She also told Joe, who I had to admit, should have been nominated for an Academy Award. He acted so surprised, not overly surprised, but just enough to appear genuine. He told Joanna he didn't want to get his hopes up in case her symptoms were due to something else. Tom was thrilled but concerned about living overseas for six months and away from home and her doctor. At first, Tom insisted on flying home with her, but we finally convinced him that he needed to get to work with Jon. We promised at least one of us would be with Joanna the entire time, and I would plan on staying with her at their home. We would take good care of her. Joe booked the additional ticket. He couldn't get seated next to ours, but at least he got one. We were set to leave England January second. I was surprised we were able to book an additional seat during the holidays. Apparently, many people stay a few days after New Year's Day, probably due to hangovers.

I had mentioned earlier to Joe that eating out was getting old. I wanted to be able to cook in my own kitchen making food that we both enjoyed. Guess I've never been much of a worldly traveler. To Joanna's and my amazement, Tom and Joe had arranged through Jon to have a catered meal delivered to the bungalow as an "eat-in"

Christmas dinner. We were delighted! We stayed in our pajamas all day. Before breakfast we opened gifts. Tom and Joanna loved the gifts from Burberry and said we spent way too much money on them, after all, Joanna pointed out we were retired and living on a fixed income. Their gift to each other was the trip. The kids had bought our gift in the states, and it was packed in their suitcase. Both Joe and I got teary-eyed after we unwrapped their gift. It was a silver plaque that was engraved. The first line read, *The Importance of Your Lives in Our Lives.*" Listed below, in chronological order, were the dates and events of our lives together.

First it listed Joe's birthdate, and then mine. It listed the date we met, our first date, and our wedding date. I couldn't believe Joanna would know those dates. Following, were the dates of Joanna's birth, her baptism, her graduation from Nursing School, and her marriage. At the end of the list was the date of Joe's and my retirement. The plaque was large enough for additional lines to be added. At the very bottom of the plaque was etched, *"Our lives would not be anything without you."*

Joanna explained they left space for adding future events, like our grandchildren's birth dates. It was so beautiful, and I'm sure expensive with all the engraving and the size of the silver plaque. It would always be treasured by us. This would not be hung in the hallway like our mirror. This would be hung in the living room where everyone would see our greatest achievement, our family.

Joe and I exchanged gifts next. Laughter abounded when we opened our gifts at the same time. Somehow Joe had purchased the same scarf for me! All four of us now owned the classic Burberry scarf. Joe said he had no idea I had bought him the same, but I think he did.

Once all the gifts were opened, Joe said, "Oh, my goodness! I forgot one more gift." He was smiling that devious smile of his. Out of the pocket of his robe, he pulled out a light teal colored box. He handed it to me saying, "Don't get mad at me for getting this for you. I had to. Selfishly, it made me feel better for not believing what you had been telling me all along. I will never doubt you again."

I was shocked looking at him. "This looks like a Tiffany box. We can't afford anything like that!"

Joanna interrupted asking, "Dad, what are you talking about?"

When he didn't answer her. She turned to me and asked, "Mom, what's going on? What's Dad talking about?"

Joe took my hand in his and turned to the kids. "Joanna and Tom, I think it's time to tell you about that mirror in our house. First, let your mother open her gift."

I was at a loss for words. My hands trembled as I opened the box. Inside was a beautiful 18 karat gold necklace with a gold infinity symbol. Several small diamonds completely outlined the infinity loop. It was stunning! I held it up and looked at Joe. I didn't know what to say.

Joe took the chain and placed it around my neck. "I hope you like it Anna. It is a symbol of our never-ending love. I love you forever and always."

My fingers felt the beautiful infinity symbol. Tears started escaping from my eyes. Then I heard louder crying. It was Joanna. She looked at both of us saying, "This is so romantic!"

That did it! We laughed and Joe said, "Let's have breakfast."

What a blessing my life was.

▪▪▪

After breakfast was eaten and the dishes cleaned up, we went into the living room to finally tell Joanna and Tom everything we had experienced with the mirror. Tom always thought the noise was something that could be explained, something maybe in the metal. He was in for a surprise.

I started the conversation off by explaining to them the day Joanna called me about the Christmas trip. She had questioned what was wrong and I told her, "Nothing." Well, I now told her about how the image appeared in the mirror and how this spirit spoke with me. Both Joanna and Tom looked at Joe at the same time with their mouths agape.

Joe smiled and put his arm around my shoulders saying, "I must admit, I thought my wife was losing her mind! So, I thought a trip away from the house would be just what she needed. She needed to get away from the mirror. You see, the mirror could not be removed from the wall. Anyone who tried to remove it felt heat and received a jolting shock. Like you, Tom, I felt the sound and heat had to be explainable. Maybe when we took the poem out of the back of the mirror we didn't look closely enough. Maybe there was some kind of battery in the mirror, but once we removed the poem and put the mirror back up, we could not take it down. I believed that until one night, Henry and his son Phillip came over. We heard noises and ran to the hallway. Anna was communicating with the spirit. She was actually talking with Annabelle."

Joanna shrieked and raised her voice at us as she asked, "Annabelle. Did you say Annabelle?"

"Yes honey," I tried to calm her down. "What's wrong?"

Suddenly she got up and said she would be right back. She ran into the bedroom and came out with a notebook. She was literally shaking.

"Mom, Dad. I have to show you something. Tom, I haven't even told you about this. This is a notebook I bought at the airport when we were leaving. I wanted it to be my 'travel journal' during our stay here. I recorded where we went sightseeing, what we ate, and where we shopped. Once I started not feeling too good, remember I was also having strange dreams?"

Joanna looked directly at me and I nodded. "Let me read what I wrote a few days ago:

'I don't know why I started getting sick today. After I threw up in the morning, I felt better. What if I'm pregnant! No, I don't think so, however, that was a strange dream last night. It was about a lady whispering to me in the wind. I assumed, in my dream, that she was dead as she was whispering from above a cloud. She was saying to name the child 'Annabelle'. I thought, 'what an old name' but she was begging me to do so." Joanna stopped reading and looked at each one of us.

Tom was the first to respond, "Honey, that is downright weird, but it was just a dream."

"Why would it be the same name, Annabelle," Joanna argued. "Mom, what do you think?"

Joe and I looked at each other. He didn't know what to say. I felt goosebumps on my arms and tried to choose my words carefully. I didn't want to upset Joanna if she was pregnant. "Joanna and Tom, a year ago I would have agreed with Tom. What we have been through the last few months, I cannot explain. I now believe spirits do exist. I never experienced any life-force or lost soul contact by anyone — not my parents, or my grandparents, that I didn't really know, no one, except Annabelle. I'm wondering, if, for decades she has wanted the truth to be told. Maybe she tried and couldn't break through, until now. Somehow, she must have attempted reaching out to the St. Martins for validation, but didn't break through. She broke through to me and that is why I feel she must be related to us, somehow. I know it all sounds absurd."

All four of us sat silent for quite a while. Joe was the first to break the silence. "It is Christmas. We cannot let a beautifully catered —and expensive — meal go to waste. Anna, you have done the majority of work in this research. How about we all just take a few breaths and relax. No one has gotten hurt over this. I suggest after dinner all four of us help Anna by diving into the remaining letters and journals Nathaniel and Catherine left with us. Maybe we can find the name of Annabelle someplace."

We all agreed but, even during our delicious meal, we were unusually quiet. We were all lost in our thoughts and fears of someone from the beyond trying to contact us. Things we never even believed in were all coming to fruition. Together the four of us put the food away and cleaned up the kitchen.

Tom gave Joanna a hug and said, "Honey, I don't want you getting upset over this. Maybe in your dream, you misunderstood. Maybe the name was 'Anna' after your mother, not 'Annabelle'."

"Tom, I know what I dreamt." Joanna sounded hurt.

 The table was now cleared off. Joe brought over the remaining letters and journals we had not yet perused. I wished I had a CD player or radio or something to play Christmas music to lighten the mood. In addition to Annabelle and Richard's names, I had instructed everyone to look for my great-grandmother's name, Margaret Smith, and anything that had reference to The Foundling Home.

After about an hour, Joe spoke up with, "Oh my God!"

In unison, we all bellowed, "What?!"

"It's in this letter to Richard's mother, Genevieve."

I shot out of my chair and stood behind Joe as he read aloud,

"Dear Genevieve St. Martin,

I am so very sorry to hear of the passing of your son, Richard. Yes, I knew my daughter, Annabelle, was with child. Her father and I have been so distraught over the unfortunate situation. I am sure you and your husband have suffered as much embarrassment with the situation as we have. I can only pray that God will forgive the souls of both Richard and Annabelle for the sins they have committed. As a family, we could not condone such conduct and have therefore placed our daughter in a home for unwed mothers where she will work until the birth of the baby. The home will not allow her to remain after the baby is born. The baby will be given up for adoption. As for Annabelle, I sincerely pray she will seek forgiveness from the Lord and find her way. She is no longer welcome in our home.

Mrs. Robert Sinclair"

Poor Annabelle. Her family disowned her, her fiancé was killed in the war, and she was more or less held prisoner in a home for unwed mothers. Deep in thought, I pondered if that was where Annabelle was in my dream. I thought maybe she had been in a palace or someplace where she worked for Queen Victoria. I was wrong. She most likely was scrubbing floors in this home when she gave birth. Then there was the poem. Somehow, she had gotten that from Richard and hidden it in the mirror. Any reference in that poem that I thought would be toward royalty was indicative of Richard's service in the war and duty for Queen Victoria. Pieces were starting to fall into place, but still, how was Nathaniel St. Martin related to me? I decided to recap on paper my suspicions of these bygone events. As I read it to Joe, Tom, and Joanna, we all confirmed the next step would be to visit the Foundling Home. We now knew that Annabelle's surname was Sinclair. I looked the name up on the internet, and it indicated the name was more French than English. There was no envelope or return address we could find for the cruel and heartless letter from Mrs. Sinclair. We would start with visiting The Foundling Home tomorrow. Anyone who had known the family would most likely be long deceased, however, I felt a hunch that something there would trigger another clue.

Chapter Twenty-Nine

It was Christmas evening. I hated to call the St. Martin's during the holiday, but in two days would be our trip on the Chunnel into France, and I wanted to get to The Foundling Home tomorrow.

Nat answered the phone and I briefly explained to him what we had discovered. He couldn't believe it! He was talking to me on the phone and relaying information to Catherine in the background at the same time.

He was indeed excited as he reassured me, "Anna, don't ever think you were insane! You did have a premonition or a spiritual visitor!"

He sounded so gleeful I had to laugh. Then, I asked if he and Catherine would join us on our trip to The Foundling Home, which was now a museum. Of course, they would. They had been there before but it was some time ago.

The next morning the St. Martins arrived in an Uber van, which had enough room for all of us. The Foundling Home Museum was located in Brunswick Square, about an hour's drive from our bungalow. My first impression of the museum was a lonely and cold feeling. It had your typical hospital-like appearance, a three-story building with a brown, brick façade. The windows had both screens and bars on them. No flowers or adornments whatsoever. It gave me the shivers. As we entered the building, a woman greeted us and handed out brochures which gave a history of the building. Built in the 1700's, it was the inspiration of philanthropist, Thomas Coram. Due to wide-spread poverty at that time and a high number of impregnated, unwed women, many abandoned babies were left on doorsteps and streets. Coram wanted to provide an establishment to take in those babies and place them in homes where families could afford to feed and care for them. The museum held tours, for a donation towards children's charities. Part of the remodeled hospital was now an art museum. I told our greeter that we were interested in a tour of the older part. After taking our donations, she turned us over to another volunteer.

Amy, our tour guide, seemed to be in her early twenties and sounded quite knowledgeable for her age. We started our tour on the third floor. Amy led us into rooms with single, narrow beds. These rooms held the women during their first six months of pregnancy. The rooms were barren with no cheerful décor whatsoever. There were twelve rooms on this floor and only one bathroom to share. After the very early 1900's, unwed mothers were no longer taken in, so there was no need to upgrade or add additional bathrooms. After six months of pregnancy, the women were moved to the first floor so they wouldn't need to climb stairs.

We moved down to the second floor. This was the nursery floor. There were two large rooms. Amy explained that each room held babies from newborn to two years old. One room was for boys and one for girls. Upon reaching two years of age, the children were moved across the hall to a dorm-like setting. Again, one area for boys and one for girls. I didn't see any play areas. The children were not to be kept in this facility past the age of nine. If they were not adopted by then, they were put to work wherever they were needed in the town, and their employer would provide them with a room.

"Amy, that is so sad. How could anyone expect a child to take care of themselves at nine years old?" I was appalled.

"It was a different time. If you've ever read the book or seen the play <u>Oliver Twist</u>, it really was like that back then, with so many children who were beggars or con artists from living on the streets." Everyone in our group seemed to be shaking their heads, imagining the unimaginable.

These rooms were similar to the ones upstairs, however, there were small dressers with basins along the wall. Above each basin was a mirror — a mirror that resembled my mirror. We all saw it. My family stood there looking at me wondering what to do or say.

"Did you have a question?" Amy inquired.

I was not shy about asking questions and Amy seemed not to mind. "Those mirrors, please tell me about them," I inquired.

"Those are antiques now. Years ago, when the girls stayed here, that was the only way they could see themselves. The history is Queen Victoria gifted twelve mirrors to The Foundling Home when

Thomas Coram built it. They aren't very pretty but they are all silver and now worth a lot of money. We now only have ten remaining, as you can see."

I tensed up. "What do you mean? What happened to the other two?"

"I'm not sure. Maybe they were stolen or they could have broken and were thrown out. It could be back then no one knew their value."

I decided to leave that one alone as I knew exactly where the other two were. One was broken in Nathaniel's mother's trunk, and the other one was attached to my wall.

"Everything seems so cold and bare. Not what you would want for nurturing yourself or your baby," I commented looking around the room.

Amy nodded and responded, "I can't imagine staying here back then or even now. I've heard stories of the treatment given since the inception of the home, and it wasn't good. I mean, the founder, Thomas Coram, had wonderful intentions, however, the care provided was only as good as the staff employed. Like I said, 'I've heard stories.'"

"Amy, is there any record of the women who were housed here, years ago or maybe centuries ago?" I probed.

"There are some old, hand-written registers from the past. They are locked in glass cases on the first floor. We will go by there, so I can show you."

The first floor was the last part of our tour. Huge doors opened up to a birthing area / operating room. Old utensils were on display. Of course, it seemed archaic for now but it must have served its purpose in the 1700's and 1800's. Amy explained that the kitchen and laundry areas were located in the basement but that was not part of the tour. On this main floor there were rooms for some staff and midwives who may need to spend the night. These rooms were much larger and nicer than the ones on the third floor. Walking toward the front of the building, Amy led us to several display cases holding historic pieces. It was a large room and as Amy explained, was used more as a reception area. I noticed the tiled floor. It was beautiful and resembled the floor in my dream! I knew it couldn't be the same floor from the 1800's but this was the one in my dream. Is this where Anabelle gave birth and lost her life? I wondered.

"This is where we display those records that you were inquiring about. I will let all of you spend some time here. If you have any questions, I'll be right around the corner in my office."

We thanked her and offered her a tip. She refused the tip saying any money we wanted to give should be in the form of a donation for the children.

I couldn't wait to get over to those cases and look at what was displayed. There were articles written about Thomas Coram and the building of The Foundling Hospital. Names of mid-wives and nurses were recorded with everything hand-written.

After about twenty minutes, I found Amy. I asked, "Do you have names of the women who stayed here and gave birth?"

"No. In the 18th and 19th centuries, families were ashamed of their children who were unmarried and pregnant. It was quite scandalous, and everyone remained anonymous. The families paid the hospital for this secrecy."

"Times have certainly changed," I remarked.

I must have seemed disappointed. Then, Amy suggested, "I can show you the names of the help back then. Let me unlock the case for you, but I ask that you don't handle the records. I have gloves you may use to turn the pages if you want."

"Thank you, Amy. I would like to see that."

We all stood around the case. Everyone remained quiet, except me. It was like they were all holding their breath. Amy put on her gloves, unlocked the case, and pulled out a record of employees' names and dates. It was hand-bound with string.

"Any particular dates you want to look at? Do you think you might know of someone who could have been related to you?"

Hesitantly I replied, "Yes, I do. I'm not sure exactly how, so I'm looking at anything that can be a hint to me."

There weren't any records from the 1700's. There were ones from the early 1900's and many names from the 1800's.

"Could you possibly find a page or two that shows workers from 1837 or thereabouts?"

Amy carefully turned the yellow, parched paper page by page. Not all of the names remained visible, fading through time. On the third page, I saw it! Emma Brown. Her name was there as clear as could be!

"That's it! Joe, I found it! That is the name Annabelle told me. The one who took her baby!"

They all gathered around to see the hand-written name.

"Amy, I know it's impossible but would anyone know anything about this person? Is her family still around?" I knew I sounded overly excited, but I was!

"Let me check with the manager."

It only took a few minutes and Amy came back with Jennifer, her manager. "How may I help you?" Jennifer asked.

I explained how I had hoped to find some connection to my family through relatives of Emma Brown and a baby that was born at The Foundling Home in 1837.

"Our records are strictly confidential as far as any children born and adopted from this facility," she stated.

"What about the workers? I am looking for anyone who may have been related to Emma Brown." I know I sounded like I was pleading with her but I hadn't gone this far to give up now.

"Brown is such a common name," Jennifer said. "I'm sorry. I don't think I can help you."

Dejected, I thanked both Jennifer and Amy for their time. We left the building as I did not feel like walking through the art that was on display. We stood outside and called an Uber for pickup.

As we were waiting, Amy came out to us. She was speaking low, almost in a whisper. "I'm so sorry for my manager's impersonal behavior. She really can be a bitch!"

We all smirked. Amy continued, "I know for a fact that there has always been a member of that Brown Family working here generation after generation."

"Are you kidding me?" I was trying to keep my voice low as I knew Amy was divulging information she may receive a reprimand for. "Do you have any idea where these relatives live?"

"Yes, I'm kind of related. A distant cousin. Being as young as I am, I'm not sure about the Emma you are searching for as they have had a few relatives with that name. I think you should ask the family. They live over on Oxford Road, about 15 kilometers from here." Fifteen kilometers was almost ten miles.

"Amy, thank you so very much."

"Promise me you won't let anyone here, especially Jennifer, know that I gave you this information," she pleaded.

Just then our Uber driver arrived.

"I promise. Do you know the exact address?" I asked.

"No, but your driver should be able to look it up."

*   *   *

Once we all packed into the Uber van, Nat asked the driver if he could look up the address for the Brown Family on Oxford Road. While we waited, Nat voiced concern if the Browns would be overwhelmed with all six of us showing up. Who knows? They may not even let us in to talk with them. Joe suggested we all take the car to the Browns and maybe Nat, as a native Londoner, could go to the door with a brief explanation of his search, mentioning Richard. If the Browns were open for a discussion, he would ask them if they would be open to discussing it with all of us, otherwise, we needed to be respectful of their privacy and leave.

Our Uber driver had no problem getting the address. It helped that we knew it was on Oxford Road about fifteen kilometers away.

The five of us remained in the car as Nat walked up the cobblestone path to the small one-level older cottage-type home. I said a prayer, begging to find the truth and to validate it in Annabelle's defense. Nat seemed to be at the door for a while before

162

turning around and starting back to the car. Half way back he turned around as an elderly woman opened the door. Moments later, Nat returned to the car letting us know that we were all welcome inside. We paid the Uber driver and cautiously went to the door. Nat whispered to us that he explained about Richard and let her know Amy said she may be willing to speak with us.

We entered the charming home that looked as though it was right out of the 1920's. The woman's name was Evelyn. She welcomed all of us into her living room, "How nice to have so many of you come and visit me. I am all alone now, and I do get company from my neighbors sometimes but, my main entertainment these days is the tele."

"We are sorry to intrude," I said. "We have been working on our family trees and came across some information of a possibility that we could be related."

"Oh, my!" she exclaimed. "I will try to help you in any way I can, but the memory isn't what it used to be. Let me first get all of you some tea."

"Please don't go to any bother. We promise not to stay long." I didn't want to inconvenience her in any way.

"Nonsense, my dear. I'm eighty-four years old, I'm not dead yet!" she chuckled.

"Then let me help you." I followed her into the kitchen where I was amazed at the delicate, flowered china cups and saucers, gingham checked curtains, and appliances that seemed like time had stood still in this little home outside of London. An old tea kettle heated water on the dated stove. I knew Joe and Tom weren't crazy about tea, but out of respect, I would never suggest anything else. I poured the hot water into each cup while Evelyn gathered cream, sugar, and honey onto a silver tray. Out of a kitchen drawer, she gathered little golden demitasse spoons. They were so cute and delicate. I was certain she hadn't used them in years. You could tell she was thrilled to have company. I asked if we should sit at the table in case of a spill in the living room.

"Don't be silly, my dear. Once you are my age, you'll realize it doesn't matter. I am just so thankful for company. I get so lonely."

I carefully carried cups into the living room, and Joanna came in to help me.

After everyone was settled, Evelyn began, "First of all, tell me all your names and where you reside."

After all the introductions had been made, Evelyn put down her teacup and asked straight forward with a serious look, "Now tell me what you really want to know."

I explained that our visit to London was with our daughter and son-in-law who was doing work with the University, however, after a DNA test, Nathaniel's name appeared on a family tree as one of my possible relatives. Evelyn didn't say anything. Then, Nathaniel spoke. Thank God for Nathaniel and Catherine! I think because they were originally from England, Evelyn trusted them more than she did us.

Nat started off by telling Evelyn how his Mum had passed last year, and while cleaning out her things, they came across an old trunk with letters and journals. In these pieces of old correspondence, the name Richard St. Martin tied into a relationship in 1837 with a young woman named Annabelle who must have died in childbirth.

"None of these names sound familiar to me," Evelyn said, yet she was in deep thought.

"You say this Richard was in a relationship with a girl that died giving birth?"

Nat nodded.

"Back then, if a girl was pregnant and not married, they were sent to a 'Home'," Evelyn continued. "My family told many sad stories of young girls dying in childbirth. There were also those who begged to keep their babies but were forced to give them up. Families disowned them, it was a wretched time."

I took up the conversation then. "Yes, Evelyn. That is where the Brown Family comes in." You see, the girl who had the baby resided at The Foundling Home, and she had a friend working there with the name of Emma Brown."

"I'm not surprised. Many of the Browns worked there from time to time, before the home turned into a museum. Yes, the women in my family, before me that is, were all mid-wives."

Evelyn had a puzzled look on her face like she was trying to remember something.

We finished our tea and Joe suggested we should probably call for the car.

Just then Evelyn said, "Wait a minute! You know, I think there was an Emma Brown involved with some sort of scandal. Yes, I remember my mother talking about it. Of course, that was so many years ago when I overheard the conversation, and I wasn't even born when it happened. It was about how she went missing. I think Emma had been my mother's cousin or something like that. I remember my mother saying how The Foundling Hospital accused Emma of stealing a baby. I don't think that was ever proven, and Emma simply disappeared. Back then, there were so many orphaned children, they most likely didn't even follow up with the missing baby."

I knew this had to be the link! "Evelyn, didn't the Brown family try to find Emma? I can't imagine her mother and father not searching for her."

"Yes, there was something. Oh, I wish I could remember. It's times like these with my fleeting memory, I know I'm old."

I felt sorry for Evelyn. It was clear from the look on her face she was trying so hard to remember. "It's all right, Evelyn. We're not here to stress you out. You've already given us more information than we had. We should let you rest now. Thank you so much for allowing us to come into your home and have tea. If you do remember anything else, maybe you could contact Nathaniel and Catherine. We will be gone all day tomorrow sightseeing, taking the Chunnel into France. I've always wanted to see Paris."

Evelyn smirked at that remark. "Believe me, Paris is not what you think. It's a dirty city."

We all laughed. I told Evelyn we would be leaving England January second, and I would love to see her again. However, we may not have time on this visit. She was delighted we stopped by and invited us all to come back whenever we could. Nat wrote down his phone number.

Chapter Thirty

It didn't take long for the car to arrive. Our driver was Scotty, the same one who brought us there. The six of us agreed we enjoyed our visit with Evelyn.

I couldn't help but remark with a smile as to the décor of her home. "It was like stepping back in time."

Joanna agreed and commented, "Mom, there is a connection there. We need to find out where Emma took that baby. That baby must have been Annabelle and Richard's baby!"

Sadly, I mentioned, "And what about Annabelle? What happened to her? Where would she be buried?"

Scotty overheard us and inquired if we were looking for someone who had passed.

Nathaniel said, "Yes, but it was long ago. She was a resident at The Foundling Hospital. She died in childbirth."

"Oh," Scotty said. "If she died while at that home, her grave could be in one of the pauper's fields unless her family arranged for burial elsewhere."

"Pauper's fields?" I questioned. "There are more than one?"

"Yes. The UK has a total of seven. They are referred to as The Magnificent Seven."

We chuckled thinking of the movie.

"Not anything to do with the movie," Scotty laughed with us. "Sometimes I work as a tour guide. The seven cemeteries were built over a period of ten years during the mid 19th century. All seven are just outside London. Prior to the inception of these seven cemeteries, those who died in London were almost always buried in small churchyards. London's population grew so much during the 18th and 19th centuries, London and its graveyards were overcrowded. I'm not sure you want to hear the rest of this history as it's kind of gruesome."

We all spoke at once, telling Scotty we wanted to know.

"OK. The graveyards were becoming so overcrowded, it began to impact the quality of life for all Londoners. Decaying matter started to seep into London's water supply and cause epidemics. Bodies were buried shoulder to shoulder, sometimes on top of each other. In 1832, British Parliament finally passed a bill to establish the building of the seven cemeteries over ten years."

"Wow!" Joanna said. "You are a fountain of knowledge."

Scotty reached into his glove compartment and pulled out a brochure of The Magnificent Seven. "You can keep this. It shows pictures of all seven cemeteries and describes their history."

We should have hired you, Scotty, to help us in our journey." I was impressed with him.

"I'm available whenever you need me."

I looked at Nat. "We are leaving for the US January 2nd, but Nat may want to follow up with you if we need additional information," I suggested.

Tom decided to get into the conversation. "Scotty, how would one find what cemetery a person would have been buried in? From my limited knowledge of pauper's fields, there are usually unmarked graves."

"That's true in many cases," Scotty replied, "but remember, these seven were built out of necessity due to the churchyards being overcrowded. The seven are actually considered 'private cemeteries' and those that could afford to would pay and even supply headstones. Each of the seven cemeteries has an area referred to as 'The Pauper's Field." Back in the 1800's, they were considered unconsecrated graves where outcasts were buried. Outcasts would have been prostitutes, criminals, people living in extreme poverty or in institutions such as The Foundling Home, if parents didn't claim their children."

"I had no idea there was such a population problem that far back in London," Joe said.

"How awful that a mother and father would not claim their own dead child!" I knew I sounded mad, but I was shocked. I wanted to know more and to try to find Annabelle's grave.

"Scotty," I probed further, "how would we find someone's grave from back then? If they were buried in the pauper's field, most likely there would be no grave marker."

"If their name was known, there was a council back then that did keep records. Otherwise, they would simply be listed as a John or Jane Doe. Do you know what year this person died?"

Joe replied, "We believe she passed in 1837."

Scotty whistled. "That is a long time ago. I think it would have to be one of two cemeteries. The first one built was Kensal Green. It was built in 1832. The second one, West Norwood, was built in 1837. You could start with those. It might take a while for clerks at the cemetery to locate the records."

I was getting impatient and edgy. "Time, time! I wish we had more time!"

Joe put his arm around me to calm me down. "Come on honey, we've already learned so much, and Nathaniel and Catherine are willing to keep looking. Maybe we should all take a break and eat something."

It was late in the afternoon, and none of us had eaten lunch. We didn't realize how starved we were.

"Scotty," Joe said, "Would you take us to a nice place for lunch? And we want you to join us. It's our treat."

"I'm all for that, and you can pick my brain a little more if you want."

Scotty was a good guy and very helpful and knowledgeable.

"What kind of food would you like? Do you like Fish 'n Chips?" Scotty knew of many restaurants, but as our driver, wanted us to be happy.

I spoke up right away, "I have to admit, Scotty, I did not care for London's Fish 'n Chips."

Joe suggested we go to a nice place with good food so this meal would serve as both our lunch and dinner.

"Scotty, are your married? Do you need to get home soon?"

"No, Joe, I'm divorced. I started doing the Uber thing as the tour guide business is so unpredictable. You know, you gotta make a living."

"Ok, then Scotty. Take us to a nice place. Maybe one that makes a good steak."

Scotty told us he knew just the place!

"We will go to The Blacksmiths Restaurant, although it's a little expensive."

"No problem," Joe said.

The Blacksmiths Restaurant was the nicest place we had been to so far in England. We were early enough to beat the evening crowd. Joe, Tom, and I indulged in a crisp gin and tonic.

Nat and Catherine decided on a light Chardonnay. Joanna, just in case she was pregnant, settled for water with lemon. Being a professional, Scotty also had water. Joe told him to go ahead and have an ale, but Scotty said no. I liked him even better.   Joe and Nat ordered the slow roasted rib eye steak. I had never heard a steak referred to as "slow roasted". All three of the women requested the pan-fried sea bass, and Scotty convinced Tom to order what he was ordering, the Blacksmiths Special Shepherd's Pie. The steak and sea bass came with truffle and wild mushroom risotto, which was delicious. The vegetable served was asparagus with poached egg. I never thought of putting those two together. I'm still not sure I liked it. Taking our time, we all ate heartily but still opted for Crème Brule dessert and were thrilled that good coffee was available and not just tea.

While enjoying dessert and coffee, Scotty said, "The Kensal Green Cemetery, the first one built in 1832, is not far from here if you are interested in visiting."

We were all getting sleepy from such a wonderful, filling meal, but I didn't know when we would have time to go to the cemetery before we had to fly home. I voiced my desire to see if we could find Anabelle's grave.

"If we go, we should leave now," Scotty said, "as the cemetery will close in an hour."

Joe picked up the tab and refused any offer to help with it. We all piled into the van and headed toward The Kensal Green Cemetery. When we arrived, I was pleasantly surprised as it was a beautiful place. Trees and flowers graced the grounds, even the

'Pauper's Field' area. The upkeep of this old cemetery was outstanding. Scotty lead us to a small chapel inside the gates. He explained to the associate working what we wanted. It would take time for him to get those old records. Some had been converted onto micro-fiche, but that would still take time to look up. I was hoping it would all be computerized. We gave him the information that we had on Annabelle.

He was a nice older man, probably retired and volunteering on this job. His name was Russell, and when I told him we had to leave after New Year's, he promised to get back to us as soon as he could. Joe gave him his phone number and so did Nat. We would have to wait. Before we left for the bungalow, I wanted to walk through the Pauper's Field area. Joe went with me, and we walked hand in hand, as did Nat and Catherine. Tom and Joanna stayed with Scotty back at the van. I suspected Joanna was too tired. Walking through this area, most of the graves were unmarked. It was so wonderful that the groundskeepers kept this isolated area just as full of foliage as the rest of the cemetery. I would have sworn as I walked along these graves, I could once again hear Annabelle, so clearly telling me to "find the link".

Exhausted, we all returned to the bungalow, thanking Scotty for his time and knowledge. I know Joe tipped him quite generously. We went to bed early, as tomorrow would be our trip to France.

Chapter Thirty-One

I was happy Jon joined us along with his parents, Nat and Catherine. We hadn't spent enough time with Jon, but he had been busy. After the holidays, Tom would be spending the majority of his time with Jon, so I knew it was a good idea that Joanna was coming back home with us for a while. She had gotten sick again this morning. It really seemed like morning sickness, but we would soon find out for sure.

Jon had advised all of us to wear comfortable shoes for walking. He said in Paris, as well as other areas of France, there would be lots of walking. Joanna was feeling better now. To our surprise, when the St. Martins arrived to pick us up, the driver was once again, Scotty. I wondered if he was one of the few Uber drivers who owned a van big enough to fit all 6 or 7 of us. He thanked us once again for dinner the previous night.

I must agree with everyone who tried to calm me down about riding on the Chunnel. They were right. Remembering how nervous I was, it was nice to see such a plush train setting inside. Seats were quite comfy and roomy. Once the train started, all I could think of was what would happen if ocean water rushed in and we all drowned. Although Joe had made fun of me, he did sit beside me and held my hand. I understood the Chunnel went quite fast, but it didn't really feel like it. I kept looking out the window to see water. I never did. I never even knew at what point we were under water.

Once we arrived in Paris and got off the Chunnel, my only comment was, "Well, that was no big deal!" Everyone laughed.

Oh, how I've always wanted to see Paris! Our walking tour, with Jon as our guide, began by visiting a perfume factory right in the middle of the shopping district. Here you could purchase brand names at wholesale cost, but there was a limit. My friends back home, as well as myself, loved Chanel #5, so I picked up a few smaller bottles as gifts. With so many well-known designers who originated from Paris, I was expecting a lusher setting. From what I observed, most places we stopped at were kind of insignificant buildings, and older shops were in need of repair.

Our next stop was the famous Louvre. Now that was an awesome structure! Standing outside looking at the massive glass triangle, I could not imagine how it was built. This pyramid had to have been assembled with such extraordinary precision. I couldn't help but see myself as part of the Tom Hanks movie "The Da Vinci Code" in search of The Holy Grail and discovering Christianity's Secret Society. Inside, I was awestruck at the "Venus de Milo" sculpture and such iconic paintings by the Great Masters. The painting of "Mona Lisa" had to be the one most people wanted to see. Surprisingly, the painting itself was much smaller than I had ever imagined.

Time to see the Eiffel Tower and then stop for lunch and hopefully take time to rest our achy feet. Even with comfortable shoes, walking on the hard cobblestone streets was not for the weak or the average senior citizen. I was happy we toured the Eiffel Tower. It was a structure everyone wanted to see. I don't know if that is a point of interest I would visit again, but I would go back to The Louvre. Jon told us the Eiffel Tower was much more impressive at night when it was lit up. I don't want to say I had been disappointed in Paris, but Evelyn was right. It was kind of a dirty city. Several times we passed the train system, referred to as "The Metro" and there was an unpleasant odor as well as many homeless people congregating. Glancing at the tracks, people did not seem to pay attention to the rats that would scurry along in search of food, and the rats did not seem to be afraid of the humans.

Jon wanted to give us a true experience of Paris for lunch at one of the largest open markets I had ever seen. We were to walk around and choose whatever we wanted to eat. We would then take our food and sit on the steps of The Bastille Opera House which was across the street from the open market.

I had no idea what I felt like eating. I don't think anyone did. I glanced over at Joanna and became worried as she didn't look well. She smiled to let me know she had it under control. There was an awful smell when we got close to the fish area of the market with raw fish hanging on hooks with their eyes sticking out. Joanna started having dry heaves. Joe told Tom to sit her down on the Opera House steps, and we would bring their lunch over. They both requested something "non-fishy". Joe and I settled on an assortment of cheese with crackers and fresh fruit. We also bought croissants with strawberry jam for everyone. Jon picked up a few bottles of wine. Sitting on those steps, people seemed to love the atmosphere which included all kinds of birds, including pigeons, diving for any crumb they could possibly scavenge. That sure made me appreciate the good old USA where we have so many beautiful open areas right in our own yards and parks. France did have some beautiful gardens that we passed, such as The Luxembourg Gardens, but they weren't places like we had at home where you can be by yourself with a glass or two of wine.

After lunch, Jon hailed two taxis, and we headed for the famous, rich shopping area of Champs Elysees. Now these stores were ones where I would picture Coco Chanel. Prices were so high, I could never afford anything along this beautifully manicured walk. We walked the whole length and reached The Arc de Triomphe. It was impressive, but I told Jon I wanted to buy some treasures at a more affordable place.

"All right," Jon smiled. "Our last stop before leaving is a little shopping area right in town. The shops are small and not well maintained, but they do carry gifts at a much more reasonable price than here."

That was where and when I started my treasured collection of "Limoge Boxes". I fell in love with these little intricate and beautifully detailed hand-painted boxes. They all open, and some of them have a tiny treasure inside. I knew back home these little boxes were anywhere from $200 to $500. Everything in the shop was marked in French Francs so Jon assisted me in the conversion to US dollars. I was pleasantly surprised that the boxes I wanted ranged from $89 to $150. I purchased three of the boxes and spent more than I wanted — close to $350 — but Joe told me to go ahead. Joanna also fell in love with them. She didn't buy any as she said she would be here for six months and could come back. One of my boxes was an open book with a red wine bottle affixed to it and when you opened the box, a small red bottle of wine was inside, not real wine but just a painted tiny bottle. Another one was an easel standing up so the box was taller. The easel had a replica painting of The Mona Lisa. When you opened the box, there was a little paintbrush inside. My third box was another taller one with the Eiffel Tower. It opened, but nothing was inside this one, however, a small version of the tower was hand-painted inside the box. These were small boxes, only about 1 ½ to 2 inches, so I knew they would be a good collection for me as they wouldn't take up much room. Also, I could leave them out all year, unlike the Christmas Villages. Exhausted, but thrilled with my purchases, we went back to the bungalow. We had seen so much of Paris in only one day. Now we had three days to relax before another full day on New Year's Eve, but that would be restful with an on-stage play, dinner, and fireworks.

Chapter Thirty-Two

Most of us slept in the day after our excursion through Paris. I stayed in bed past 11:00 am, and Joanna was still in bed at noon. Tom said she felt good, just tired. The guys had been up for a few hours and had already gone through one pot of coffee. They also had gone up to the bakery and come back with an entire box of donuts and croissants. I was thrilled and starved.

I consumed two donuts with my coffee, and when Joanna finally got up, I joined her for a croissant. We sat around most of the day. Later that afternoon, Nat called asking if he and Catherine could stop by later or the next day. Joe told them to come over as we weren't doing anything, just relaxing.

I was anxious for them to arrive as I wondered if they found out any additional information

I was surprised that the St. Martins already had news from Evelyn. Evelyn had contacted Nathaniel and was excited she had found more information on Emma Brown. Apparently after we left, Evelyn kept thinking about something she knew happened but couldn't quite remember. Nat relayed to us that she told him over the phone how she couldn't sleep, so she searched through her cedar storage chest. It had been years since she had opened it. Remembering a box of her mother's personal belongings that was stored in the chest, she pulled it out and looked through it. She found her mother's diary. Evelyn asked Nat if we could all please come over to see her as soon as possible. Of course, we said yes. Nat phoned Evelyn on his cell phone, and we headed out the door. Our driver this time was not Scotty. Maybe next time we would specifically ask for him.

Lovely little Evelyn. She was such a gracious hostess. She had already made tea for us and arranged her antique china cups along with the gold demitasse spoons. Evelyn also had a bakery box filled with scones. I wondered how she got them, as surely she no longer drove a car, and it was too far for her to walk. I didn't ask as I didn't want to waste time getting more information about Emma Brown.

Sitting in the living room, I noticed the old diary was on Evelyn's coffee table.

"I'm so glad you came over again to see me. I enjoy having company." Evelyn was sweet but, as selfish as my thoughts were, I hoped she had information and didn't just invite us over because she was lonely.

"Evelyn," I began. "Nathaniel told us you found some more information on Emma Brown."

"Oh, yes, you know after you left a few days ago, I kept trying to remember why it all sounded so familiar. I couldn't sleep. I tossed and turned. Finally, I got up and searched in my old cedar chest to see what I could find. I had kept a box of Mum's things and never really looked through all of them. Then, I found her diary! I was so excited! I felt like I was Sherlock Holmes trying to solve a mystery."

Smiling to herself, she sipped her tea without any other conversation. I looked at Nat. He nodded and took over for me,

"Evelyn, how exciting for you. I suppose it was difficult looking through some of your Mum's things. It always brings back memories, doesn't it?"

"Oh, yes. I do miss my mum."

Nat continued, "You said over the phone you had found out additional information about Emma Brown."

Slapping her hand on her thigh and laughing, Evelyn replied, "My goodness, yes. I suspect you're waiting to hear what I found out." Evelyn took a few minutes as if she was gathering her thoughts. I hoped this was information we could use.

"You see that old diary there?" She pointed to the coffee table. We nodded.

"My mum tracked down what happened to Emma. At least she knew about her and wrote it down in there. Her diary says it was what her mum, my granny, who told her. I don't know why she wrote about such things. It was a scandal, better off kept buried."

I looked around the room and all of us sat quietly with wide opened eyes. I wondered if she would not tell us. I think even Nat was not sure what to say.

I pressed on, "Evelyn, we don't want to upset you, and we would never divulge any information you share with us. We simply are trying to figure out how Nathaniel and I could possibly be related. We think it had something to do with Richard St. Martin and Emma Brown."

Evelyn grabbed the diary off the coffee table and cradled it possessively at her chest. "I won't give you the diary."

Worried she was about to cry, Nathaniel walked over to reassure her we didn't want the diary. Catherine got up to refresh Evelyn's tea.

I got up and walked over to Evelyn. I bent down and touched her shoulder, "Please know, Evelyn, we are not here to take advantage of you or any of your family's secrets. We won't even read that diary, but can you tell us what was revealed to you when you read it?"

She seemed to calm down. Nat and I returned to our seats. I could tell Evelyn was deep in thought and kind of sad. I'm sure finding that box of her mother's things brought back many memories. After all, Evelyn said she was all alone now.

We sat in silence for a while. Suddenly, Evelyn put the diary back on the table, smiled and said, "Oh, what the hell! Everyone in my family is gone. I will tell you what I know."

Evelyn was so prim and proper, so everyone chuckled at her language. Everyone, except for me. I had been holding my breath, silently praying for her to reveal what she now remembered.

We all sat quietly as Evelyn revealed the family's secret. "Emma Brown had been a mid-wife working at The Foundling Home. Emma was not an attractive woman, and at age 30 had yet to have any male companionship. Her life was her work at the Home. She befriended a young pregnant girl by the name of Annabelle Rose."

What a pretty name, I thought.

Evelyn took another sip of tea and continued. "Emma was a jealous woman. I guess maybe it was that she was unattractive, unmarried, and her parents didn't seem to help her at all. One night, Emma's friend, Annabelle, couldn't sleep and was cleaning the floors at The Home when she went into labor. It was late in the evening, so most everyone was sleeping. Emma had gotten up to go to the bathroom when she heard Annabelle's scream asking for help. Once Emma got to her, she realized there was no time left as the baby was coming. Poor Annabelle bled all over the floor, but Emma being the skillful mid-wife she was, successfully delivered Annabelle's baby. At least successful for the baby. Annabelle had lost too much blood. Maybe if someone was with her when she first went into labor, it would have worked out differently. Before Annabelle died, she begged to see her baby. It was a girl. Annabelle died on that cold floor right after seeing her baby. Emma woke up the matrons on the floor to tell them of Annabelle's death. While they took care of Annabelle's body, Emma cleaned the baby up and swaddled her. She felt so close to this child. Emma wouldn't leave to go home. She wanted to stay close to the baby."

"How do you know all these details?" Joe asked. "All that could not have been written in the diary, was it?"

"No," Evelyn replied. "Once I read my mum's account of Emma and the baby, I remembered listening to all the stories throughout the years that my family talked about."

"What happened to Emma and the baby?" I wanted more information.

"The other mid-wives at The Foundling Home were giving Emma trouble because she wasn't doing her work. She only wanted to help Annabelle's little baby girl. Poor Annabelle. Her family was notified of her death but wanted nothing to do with her or the baby. That baby apparently was in very good health and no doubt would be adopted soon. From what I remember hearing, Emma even started calling the baby 'Maggie' and believed it was her child. One night, while the baby was still an infant, both Emma and baby 'Maggie' disappeared."

Everyone was silent for what seemed to be the longest time.

"Evelyn," I quietly asked, almost in a whisper, "Did anyone ever find out what happened to them."

"After many years, Emma did contact her parents. She finally met someone and got married. He was older than she was, but she was almost 40 years old when they wed. The little girl, 'Maggie' was nine or ten by then."

"Do you have any idea who Emma married or what her last name would have been?"

"It was Swedish, I think. I can't remember. Oh, wait a minute, I think it was in my mum's diary."

I sat there so impatiently while Evelyn searched the pages of the diary. "Here it is. Oh yes, I'll read it to you. 'Emma and the baby ran off to Sweden where she knew no one would find her. Years later she met and married Arvid Svvenson.'"

Not realizing I was holding the teacup in my hand, I started shaking as the teacup fell to the floor. Tears rolled down my cheeks as Joe knelt down by my side followed by Joanna. We all knew. We knew the link had been found!

Evelyn didn't know what was going on. She told us not to worry about the tea on her floor.

I couldn't talk. Joanna chimed in, "Evelyn, that is the link. We know how mother's family tree relates to Nathaniel's. We are related!"

Chapter Thirty-Three

By the grace of God, and the help of Annabelle's "ghost", my prayers had been answered.

We stayed at Evelyn's for a few hours that night. Everyone hugged and shed a few tears, especially Nat and I. I wasn't sure Evelyn grasped the enormity of the gift she had given us. After my tears subsided, I tried to explain, as best as I could what this truth meant to me. I would never tell Evelyn about Annabelle's spirit coming into our lives. That would have been too much for her to handle. What I told her was how this unraveling explained more things than I could have imagined.

"Evelyn, I didn't know my great-grandmother, but I knew she was from Sweden. She was born in 1837 and her name was Margaret. Maggie is a nickname for Margaret. I wondered why she was Swedish when there were no blonde-haired or blue-eyed people throughout my family's history. Now I know. You see, I believe my great-grandmother was Richard St. Martin and Annabelle Rose's child." I paused, trying to remain calm and not start crying again. That would mean my true great-great-grandparents would have been Richard and Annabelle."

I was truly thrilled along with everyone else. Everyone, that is, except Evelyn. She sat in her chair with a sad expression and kept repeating, "Oh, dear. Oh, dear."

"What's wrong Evelyn?" I asked. "This is good news, isn't it?"

"I am so sorry. So sorry for all of you. So sorry my family put you through such misery for all these generations." Evelyn started tearing up. "You will never come and see me again, and you will never like me. My family was terrible to do this. I know Emma did it, but they knew and said nothing!"

Speaking all at once, we tried to reassure her. I knelt down beside her chair and Nat did the same on the other side. Nat told her how he would always visit her, explaining it wasn't her fault that so many, many years ago Emma stole this baby. The important thing was we now knew what the truth was, and he had a whole new side of his family. I followed up telling Evelyn we were leaving to go home in a few days, but I would love to come visit her one more time before I left. I then asked her if it would be OK if I wrote to her.

"Oh, that would be lovely!" she said in her proper English way. "Maybe you will come back and visit someday."

"I might just do that."

Joanna spoke up telling Evelyn she was leaving too but would be back in a week, "Would it be all right with you, Evelyn, if I come over once or twice a week to have tea with you?"

"Well, now I'm crying tears of joy." I believe Evelyn was truly happy.

Leaving Evelyn to rest as it was clearly past her bedtime, we let her know we would see her the day before New Year's Eve.

All of us were almost speechless during the ride home, each in our own thoughts. I gave Nat and Catherine a big hug goodbye, but we would see them in a few days. Once in the bungalow, I was too keyed up to sleep. Tom, Joanna, Joe, and I sat in the living room going over what would hereafter be our family tree. I had several open-ended questions, such as wondering if my great-grandmother, Margaret, ever knew who her real parents were? I suspect not. I wondered what Emma had told her about what happened to her "father". She most likely told her the truth — that he was killed in the war. How I wish I had known my great grandma, Margaret. I wanted to know what kind of childhood she had, if she was happy, and if Emma was kind to her. I wondered why it took all these years for Annabelle to break through and what would now become of her spirit? What would we do with the mirror?

Then there was my grandpa, Edward Smith. He was Margaret and Albert's child. Why did he never see his parents after he came to America? Was it because people back then did not travel that far? I could only speculate about these things.

The important thing was we had found the link, and I had new relatives in England. Distant ones, but still relatives, and now good friends. Would Annabelle know we found the link, would I need to try to communicate this through the mirror when we returned

home? Time would tell.

Chapter Thirty-Four

New Year's Eve, watching fireworks over The Thames was by far the most beautiful display of fireworks I had ever seen. The day before we visited Evelyn for the last time before we would be leaving. It was a bittersweet visit, wondering if she would still be here whenever we made our next visit. I was so proud of my daughter, knowing she would make the effort to have tea each week with Evelyn.

Going to Evelyn's that day, we requested Scotty as our driver. He was happy to see us and had some news. He had been planning on dropping by to tell us. On his day off he had gone back to the Kensal Green Cemetery. The groundskeeper had located listings of the pauper's fields graves since inception of the cemetery in the 1800's. He had the records boxed up from a cabinet in a warehouse and would hold them for a few days if we wanted to go through them. I felt as if everything had fallen into place.   We told Evelyn about it, and she wanted to go with us to the cemetery. Scotty picked us all up, and we found a street vendor selling flowers.

When we reached the cemetery office, the groundskeeper pulled the list from the 1800's. He apologized, saying he tried to get the micro-fiche copies but his machine wouldn't work. Thank goodness the lists were well-preserved. We were touching history and were so surprised we were allowed to handle such documents.

It took close to an hour, but we found a listing for Annabelle Rose. The groundskeeper led us to the numbered area that was marked in the record. Standing there, we looked down at a place on the ground where there was only a small plaque with a number identifying the grave. The cemetery had green tins that stuck in the ground for flowers. Joanna and I arranged the flowers and gently pushed the green tin into the earth that below held the remains of Annabelle Rose. I began praying The Our Father and Hail Mary out loud while the others joined in. Evelyn sobbed as she spoke to Annabelle out load asking for her family's forgiveness. As we left, I inquired if it would be possible to have a marker or headstone made. Would the cemetery be willing to put a headstone on Annabelle's grave after all these years? They would. I got some information from Russell, the groundskeeper, and told him I would be in touch. Evelyn insisted on paying for it. We finally settled on sharing the cost. That seemed to satisfy her.

We had been through so much with this trip. I felt I had put my family through enough that it was more of a "working" vacation. Tom told me not to worry. After all, they would be here for six months. Joe said it was an experience we would always hold dear. We couldn't really tell everyone everything, but we knew.

That night, I was more emotionally fatigued than physically fatigued, but I slept peacefully. In my peaceful slumber, Annabelle appeared to me. She was smiling with a glow around her as she whispered, "Thank you." Alongside her was a soldier holding her hand. I knew it was Richard. I told Joe, Tom, and Joanna about my dream. I didn't tell the others as it was just a dream, or was it?

So now it was our day of total enjoyment. Jon arranged our transportation in a limousine. What a treat! I wore the dress I brought along and felt a little underdressed, but I didn't care. Everyone made us feel so comfortable. Our first stop was at The Playhouse Theatre. Jon had gotten tickets to see "Flashdance." It was an older play but we didn't care. The dancing was incredible!

Following the performance, the limo drove us to a fancy restaurant, "Le Pont de la Tour". This restaurant, seated up close next to The Thames River, was upscale Alfresco dining. Ideal for sitting outside next to the water, it was not the season for this. However, to thoroughly enjoy the fireworks that evening, we were seated in front of huge double doors that opened up once the sky show over the river began. I thought Jon must have a lot of money as he paid for everything. The meals were delicious. We dined on prime rib, shucked oysters, and tried a few samplings from the crustacea bar. Everything was scrumptious. Just before the fireworks show started, we were each served a mouthwatering single serve, chocolate lava cake. Then came the champagne and the wishes for the best New Year ever. I felt like I was the queen. In one trip, less than two weeks long, my life had changed. I had found the historical mystery I searched for. I found new friends, and most importantly, I found family.

Epilogue

I find it hard to believe it has been more than five years ago we made that life changing journey to England. Joanna traveled home with us. Both Joe and I stayed with her at her home for a week. We were retired, so there was no need to hurry home to Minnesota. Joanna saw her doctor that week and received the wonderful confirmation of her pregnancy. She was barely two months along, so her doctor advised her not to fly after eight months, which wouldn't be a problem as she and Tom would be back home by then. She needed to see a doctor in London every month she was there, and that doctor would have to fax monthly visit reports back to her doctor in the US.

Joe and I, as well as Tom's parents went out East for the baby's arrival. Sweet beautiful Annabelle Rose entered the world with quite a wail. She was perfect. Dark hair and brown eyes graced her heavenly face. Tom's parents did not know our story and commented how Annabelle Rose was such an old name. Joanna smiled and told them she was named after a great aunt. We decided to treasure our family history. Maybe one day I would write a book about it, but for now we simply enjoy our little family and marvel at how it came about.

Presently, the five of us, Tom, Joanna, Annabelle Rose, Joe and I, are headed to England to visit Nat and Catherine. Annabelle is so excited to have her first airplane ride.

Sadly, Evelyn passed away two years after we left England. I had kept in contact with her, and I knew she was grateful for our letter exchanges. Her home was all she had, and she willed that to Nathaniel. He kept the home and fixed it up like he did with his mother's. He wanted us to stay there and maybe get all together to have a cup of tea, a toast for Evelyn, using her beloved china teacups and demitasse spoons that the St. Martins could not part with.

Five years ago, after we got Joanna back on that plane going to London and Tom, Joe and I flew home. We had no idea what to expect as to the situation with the mirror upon our return. The house was quiet, no strange sounds whatsoever. Together, we walked into the hallway toward the mirror. There was no rippling, and there was no humming. Joe placed his hands on the mirror. It was cool to his touch. He decided to be brave and see if he could remove it from the wall. Carefully he placed his hands on each side of the mirror and gently lifted it off the nail. Nothing happened. I could never explain it. Would the first Annabelle ever make an appearance again? I hoped not, as I felt reassured she and Richard had finally found peace.

That first week home, I contacted Henry, Phillip, and Mark. They came over to the house to witness that the mirror had gone silent and was removed. They sat in amazement and reverence as they listened to the unraveling of our historical narrative, proving we had communicated with Annabelle's spirit. Some force had led us through our journey. Most people wouldn't believe it, just as I didn't at first. Even Phillip didn't believe it until he witnessed Mitzi's spirit so many years ago in his father's store. Phillip and Mark offered me a very generous amount of money for the mirror. I couldn't part with it, at least not yet. Maybe someday. I no longer had any fear of the mirror, and money could not replace the wonder and miraculous events our family had experienced.

Last year, my dear friend Henry passed away. He was ninety-nine years old. The funeral took place in his hometown of Stillwater, Minnesota. Lexi, Donna, and I all attended. Many people who had purchased antiques at his store throughout the years were there. Henry was not cremated. In his own style, he chose to be buried in an antique-like, hand carved casket.

All of his collections throughout the years were still in his home. Before his death, he instructed Phillip and Mark what they should sell and what to keep. It was unbelievable the amount of wealth that was squeezed into that small, old home of his. It amounted to millions.

After the funeral service, Phillip asked me to come out to his car with him. Henry had left something for me. It was a scroll of some sort, secured with gold string. A card was attached. I opened the envelope and read the card,

"My dearest Anna,

Please forgive an old man his delight in wanting you to find your ancestry, your lineage. We are the few who know there is life after death, and I hope to someday celebrate that afterlife with you and your family. I located this provenance soon after your first encounter with Annabelle. I knew you had to have had a connection, a history together, once she appeared to you. I kept it in hopes you would pursue your own history and discover the importance of fate. I am so pleased you found it. This provenance will help you sell the mirror, if you so choose. I estimate this first and only purchase you made at my store for $300, now has a value anywhere from $33,000 to $50,000. Enjoy this life.

See you in the hereafter, your friend,

Henry"

I have framed Henry's letter along with the provenance of the mirror on our bedroom wall. It hangs next to the mirror. Joe and I chose to hang it in our bedroom as it is a story for us, not anyone who comes over.

Grandma Margaret's afghan is now encased in a large glass shadow box and hangs in our living room alongside the silver plaque from Joanna and Tom. The engraving of Annabelle Rose's name and birth has been added.

As I sit during this flight to England, I reflect on my life. Little Annabelle Rose sits beside me, getting sleepy and cuddling her little bear. Like children her age, she has too much energy for this 75-year old. Joe can keep up with her better than I can. He adores her. Yes, she is like other children, but yet, I often catch this twinkle in her eye, making me wonder if part of the first Annabelle's spirit is within her.

We all plan on visiting the cemetery during this trip to England. I want to see the headstone that Evelyn, Joe and I arranged over her grave. It will be up to Joanna and Tom if they want their child to know her history. Maybe someday, when she is much older. For now, we delight in the time we have with our little family. They still live out East. Tom and Jon work together now, mostly creating and selling art, so Tom often goes to London for business. He has been offered a full-time art history teaching job at the University in London but he's not sure he wants it; especially now that they are expecting their second child. Joanna is four months pregnant. They found out it will be a boy and decided to name him Richard. How appropriate.

Everyone is getting sleepy now on this long plane ride. I close my eyes and smile as I hear a soft echoing, "Remember, we are only a breath away."

Anna's Family Tree

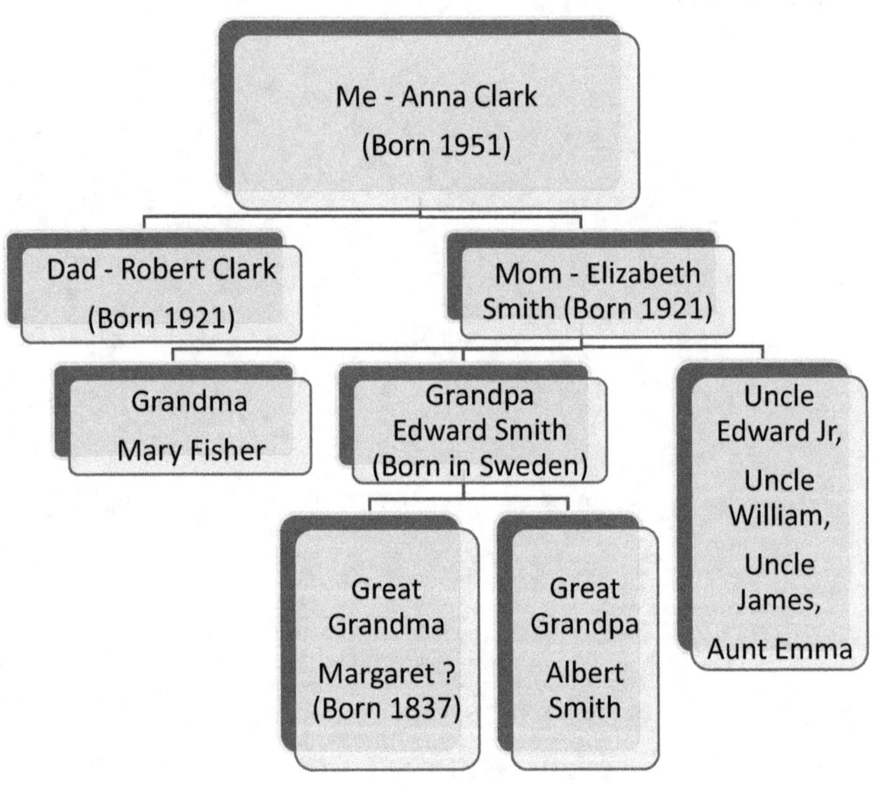

9 798634 265407